What the cri

"These are three great stories of women awakening to their hidden, erotic desires by caring, sensitive men. I really enjoyed the fact that all the women were strong, mature, and successful but still willing to experience a world of sexuality that allowed them to enjoy a new level of sensuality." – *Sharon Bressen, Sensual Romance Reviews*

About **Last Kiss** by Dominique Adair:

"Dominique Adair has written a very sensual love story that will enormously entertain the audience." - *The Best Reviews*

"5 stars" - *Sime~Gen, Inc.*

"Ms. Adair certainly knows how to create a sensual aura around her dynamic characters that sizzles and burns out of control in this well told story. This is a one sitting read!" - *reviewer Suzanne Coleburn*

"Though short in length, LAST KISS packs quite an emotional punch...while the love scenes are quite erotic, the romance between the heroine, Elaine, and the hero, Alexei, proves profound, tender and moving." - *Sondrea Cash, Romance Reviews Today*

About **Power Exchange** by Madeleine Oh:

"Author Madeline Oh pens an exciting story in POWER EXCHANGE and keeps the readers interest level high... a delightful experience." - *Michelle Gann, Romance Reviews Today*

"An enjoyable and arousing read." - author *J.Z. Sharpe*

About **Sex Magic** by Jennifer Dunne:

"A guaranteed winner for Ms Dunne and a fascinating read for every reader." - *Irene Marshall, Escape to Romance*

"An excellent story...you won't want to put down." - *Sensual Romance*

"Author Jennifer Dunne pens a fantastic tale of erotic romance sure to please and keep readers on their toes. The characters' emotions and feelings leap off the pages, pulling the reader into the story. SEX MAGIC is very graphic, and the love scenes, though graphic, are beautifully orchestrated. I look forward to reading more from this talented author." - *Michelle Gann, The Word On Romance*

Discover for yourself why readers can't get enough of the multiple-award-winning publisher Ellora's Cave. Whether you prefer e-books or paperbacks, be sure to visit EC on the web at www.ellorascave.com for an erotic reading experience that will leave you breathless.

www.ellorascave.com

Ellora's Cave Publishing, Inc.
PO Box 787
Hudson, OH 44236-0787

ISBN # 1843607433

Two Days, Three Nights, edited by Kari Berton
Power Play, edited by Sheri Carucci
Annie's Birthday Bachelor, edited by Martha Punches
Cover art by Darrell King.

TIED WITH A BOW

Written by

DOMINIQUE ADAIR, JENNIFER DUNNE, & MADELEINE OH

TWO DAYS, THREE NIGHTS

Written by

DOMINIQUE ADAIR

Chapter One

Victoria Brittain dreaded the next few hours. Tonight was Olive Street Designs' annual thank-you party for their clients. This week's work alone had heralded another major coup in signing their first million-dollar contract. Not that she wasn't happy the company was doing well because she was, but tonight she'd have traded her coveted corner office for a quiet weekend at home.

When she and her brothers had begun the advertising company just over two years ago, they'd never dreamed of making a success of their joint venture in such a short period of time. Having grown up with little money and second-hand clothing from the thrift shops down the street, they'd looked for a way to support the Brittain family and utilize the siblings' artistic creativity. But they'd never dreamed they'd hit the million-dollar mark in such a short time.

She closed her eyes and tipped back her head.

And as the head of OSD marketing, her recent bonus netted just over ten thousand dollars. A delicious thrill of anticipation ran through her as she contemplated a cruise in the dead of winter. She could just imagine sailing the warm, tropical seas and soaking up the sun while her home in New York City was blanketed by snow. The time away would be sheer bliss. No calling, faxing or paging. Her day wouldn't be interrupted with the myriad of problems that came with her high-powered profession. One whole week of naps, sunbathing and an endless supply of margaritas…

A knock on her office door interrupted her daydream and her executive assistant popped in. "This was just delivered." Kelley was carrying a white box tied with a lavish red bow.

Victoria sat up. "Who's it from?"

"No idea. Nothing is written on the outside other than our address, and it was delivered via private messenger." Kelley placed the box on the desk. "Maybe there's a card inside?"

"Could be." Victoria picked up an interoffice envelope. "Can you drop these off to legal for me?"

"Sure thing. Also, your evening wear is hanging on your bathroom door." Kelley glanced at the gold watch Victoria had given her for Christmas last year. "You have a half hour before you need to be downstairs."

Victoria nodded, her attention already focused on the box. It was roughly ten by ten and unwrapped save the large bow. A small printed label contained her name and OSD's address. As the office door closed behind her assistant, Victoria tugged on the bow and removed the lid. Nestled in a cloud of white tissue paper was a handwritten card.

Wear this tonight so that I may entertain myself

with the thought of my gift against your skin.

She fingered the heavy ivory linen cardstock as she contemplated the masculine scrawl. The card itself gave no clues. It was high quality stationery and readily available in many shops here in New York. The handwriting was unfamiliar, but in this day and age of computers and faxes, when was the last time she'd seen a handwritten note?

She sighed and dropped the card on her desk. Pawing through the layers of tissue paper, a startled squeak caught in her throat when the box's treasure was revealed.

Of the sheerest black silk, the bodice of a camisole was adorned with tiny black seed pearls, jet beads and trimmed in soft lace. Victoria lifted the camisole by the delicate ribbon straps as she marveled over the exquisite beading. A matching thong lay nestled beneath in its bed of tissue. Small lace bows and a cluster of matching pearls and beads adorned the narrow front.

She bit her lip. Who would have sent her such an intimate and extravagant gift? Obviously an attendee of tonight's party. Many men—clients, she silently amended—had been invited for the festivities this evening. Which one of them would be forward enough to send her a gift of expensive lingerie?

She eyed the delicate beading. This set had cost several hundred dollars at least. She bit her lip again. Was she daring enough to wear this gift to the party?

Could she dare not to?

Her eyes narrowed as she stroked the silk between her fingers. Mentally running through a list of her co-workers, she couldn't think of anyone who'd dare to send such an intimate gift. Around the office she had the reputation of a dragon-lady, though she was acknowledged as being fair as well as tough. None of the men who worked at OSD had ever presumed to ask her out on a date let alone hint that they were interested in her sexually.

That left clients.

And dating a client would be a disaster. End of story. She kicked off her sensible black shoes before rising from her chair. Often, behind closed doors, she'd remove her shoes while she worked. She enjoyed the feel of the plush gray carpeting beneath her feet. Taking the box with her, she headed for her private bathroom.

It was small but functional, decorated in pale gray and mauve. She laid her gift on the gleaming marble vanity and reached into the postage stamp-sized shower to turn on the water. After adjusting the temperature, she stripped off her clothes and stepped into the hot spray.

As she lathered her favorite lavender soap, Victoria began preparing a mental list of clients attending the party this evening. Of the hundred or so people, two-thirds of the responders were men and the majority were bringing dates or their wives. Not that having a woman by their side would stop many from making passes at other women.

It certainly hadn't stopped her ex-fiancé.

Victoria scowled as she rinsed the soap off her skin. Thoughts of Brad were certainly not welcome this evening. He'd left her almost a year ago when he'd found a younger, thinner more masochistic girlfriend. Not that Victoria had anything against a little pain with her sex; a gentle spanking or light bondage was a welcome change to vanilla sex. Let's face it, sex could get boring when left with the same face over and over again.

She turned off the water and flung open the shower door. Brad had left her before they'd ventured too far into the bondage and discipline world. That was probably her greatest regret over the demise of the relationship; not that Brad leaving was a loss, as that had been a blessing in disguise. Rather she'd been left with the feeling that she was definitely missing out on something spectacular. She grabbed a towel from the heated towel rack. Maybe it was time to get back into the game and find another playmate? Someone with an interest in the same style of kink she'd long suspected she'd enjoy?

She frowned. How did one go about finding a patient Dominant willing to train a potential submissive but most definitely sexual adventuress like herself? The Internet? The newspaper? She turned and caught a glance of her pale body in the mirror and her breath left her in a noisy huff.

Preposterous.

She was a thirty-seven-year-old advertising executive, not some twenty-something girl that most of her male associates seemed to look for. Maybe the gift was just a present from a grateful client with a wicked sense of humor. She turned away from the mirror and began drying herself. Granted, the usual gift consisted of a bottle of fine wine or tickets to a show, not sexy lingerie.

The open box was lying on its marble altar. The overhead light cast shadows on the silk and made the pearls glow and beads flash. The garment seemed to be mocking her attempts to find a reasonable, rational explanation for its appearance.

She tossed the damp towel over the bar. Okay, supposing the gift was from a man who desired a physical relationship with her. Who could that be? She picked up her bottle of body lotion and poured a generous amount into her palm.

Michael Walls, owner of the Walls Appliance mega-stores was a possibility. He was on tonight's guest list and he was very single, very eligible and definitely good-looking. Then there was Harry Irons, the president of Irons Gaming Software. She smiled as she smoothed lotion up her thighs. Harry might be a genius with computers but he couldn't concentrate long enough to ensure that his socks matched when he got dressed. There was no way it could have been him.

What about....

Victoria stopped.

No.

William Hunter.

His name alone caused a rebellious little flutter in her midsection. She met with him every three to six months after he'd pulled his account from a rival firm when OSD had opened its doors. It was actually Brad's connection to Hunt that had landed the very profitable account squarely in her lap. Even after OSD had expanded and she'd hired staff, Hunt had insisted she take care of his account personally rather than handing it off to a subordinate. She'd never understood why as their meetings were always short, impersonal lunches or simple get togethers in her office. William Hunter had never done or said anything to indicate he was interested in her for anything beyond managing his marketing plan.

Of course, that hadn't stopped her from imagining him naked. William Hunter was a good-looking man. Tall with dark brown hair and bedroom eyes to die for. And she respected him both as a client and as a person. He had a quick mind, a generous spirit and the fact the man could fill out a pair of jeans like no one else was an extra-added bonus.

She bit her lip as she reached for the thong panties. Stepping into them, she shivered as the cool silk skimmed her legs before settling high on her hips. She'd never worn a thong before and she glanced in the mirror to see how it looked.

For her age, she was passable. She ate well, worked out three times a week and her breasts weren't sagging too much...yet. She ran her hand over the generous curve of her left breast. She'd always been big chested and wore minimizing bras to hide what her mother had considered to be a flaw. She didn't think it was a flaw to have large breasts. She brushed her thumb over the hardened tip and a breath of air escaped her. They were pretty nice as far as breasts went and very sensitive. On more than one occasion she'd brought herself to orgasm strictly by playing with her nipples.

Regardless of how nice they were, they were still thirty-seven-year-old breasts and Hunt had been seen around town with twenty-something cover models. Victoria reached for a strapless bra. She couldn't compete with cover models so that ruled out the handsome shipping owner entirely. For all she knew her admirer was the elderly Oscar Potts, owner of a chain of automobile detailers.

She grinned as she slid the camisole over her head. She certainly couldn't imagine Oscar sending any woman a gift of such an intimate nature. Come to think of it, she couldn't imagine any of her clients sending her lingerie. So maybe it wasn't a client?

Disappointed somehow, she reached for her makeup bag. To bad it couldn't be Hunt. An affair with him could be fun, not that she'd ever mix business with pleasure, of course. His account was too important to OSD and she'd never do anything to jeopardize their financially profitable relationship.

She sighed. Scruples were a pain sometimes.

She applied a light amount of makeup and twisted her hair into a simple chignon. Already she could hear her guests arriving and it was time to get this show on the road.

Her garment bag hung on the back of the door where Kelley had put it earlier. With a quick tug on the zipper, she pulled an exquisitely tailored tuxedo jacket and matching floor-length skirt from the bag. Her sheer black thigh-high stockings were neatly folded inside one of the matching high-heeled pumps in the bottom of the bag.

Drawing the stockings up her legs, she reveled in the innate sensuality of the movement as the dangling beads on the front of the thong teased her silk-covered mound. She'd always been a sensual creature and now, thanks to her gift, she was almost painfully aware of her body. It had definitely been far too long since she'd had sex. She smoothed the stockings on her thighs, reveling in the tingling the movement awakened at the apex of her legs. This was an issue she'd have to address and soon. Maybe she'd meet a single, handsome man on the cruise? One who wouldn't be adverse to a little spanking and a lot of sex.

Stepping into the skirt, she pulled it up and zipped it at the waist. The back was slit so high that wearing a slip was impossible. She slid her feet into towering heels, smiling when they added another three inches to her five-foot-eight inch frame.

The jacket was deceptively simple with its double-breasted design. She buttoned the jacket and the deep V just barely hid the top of the camisole. Only when she bent over would the jacket part enough to allow a glimpse of silk and her ample cleavage. She gave herself a quick spritz of lavender water. Now she was ready to face the party.

A trill of naughtiness swept through her as she opened the bathroom door. Would her secret gift-giver make himself known this evening? She certainly hoped he did and could only pray he wasn't a client.

Chapter Two

Victoria sipped the excellent champagne, an interested smile pasted on her face. In all of her years in the corporate world, the parties never changed. People drank too much, ate too much and slipped off into corners and supply closets to grope people they wouldn't notice for the rest of the year.

She nodded as Ophelia Potts, Oscar's new wife, expounded on the joys of the tofu cookbook she'd received for her birthday. In reality, Victoria couldn't have cared less as she was preoccupied with uncovering the identity of her mystery gift-giver. Here it was, over two hours into the evening, and no one had so far come forward.

Michael Walls had arrived alone, but he'd paid her no more attention than usual. Other than the obligatory greeting he'd said no more. No sly smiles, no knowing looks. She mentally crossed him off her list.

Harry Irons had arrived with a brand new fiancée in tow, and with Oscar's startling arrival with Ophelia she could safely remove both of them. There were several unescorted males in the room and, while she knew their names, she'd never dealt with them personally. There was no reason to think any of them would send her the gift.

She'd seen Hunt from a distance but he'd acknowledged her presence with nothing more than a vague nod in her direction. She ignored the sinking feeling in the pit of her stomach. A man with his money, looks and connections could have any woman to warm his bed. There was no reason to send Victoria anything when he had a bevy of beautiful young models to pick from.

Victoria jerked as she realized Mrs. Potts was tugging her arm. "I'm sorry, what did you say?"

The other woman gave her an odd look. "Are you okay? You looked like you were a million miles away."

"I'm sorry, Mrs. Potts." She waved her hand to encompass the crowded atrium. "I'm afraid I'm getting quite a headache. Maybe I can slip up to my office and take something."

The older woman nodded and patted her arm. "You do that, dear. Take some aspirin and have a few quiet moments."

Victoria smiled and left her half-full champagne glass on a tray of used stemware. Sneaking off for a breather was a great idea. Nothing sounded better than kicking off her torturous heels and sitting for a few minutes. She made her way to the stairs, expertly dodging employees and clients alike who wished to detain her for a few words.

She reached the second floor balcony and looked over the railing at the milling throng. Nowhere did she see Hunt. Had he left already?

She ignored the sting of disappointment at the thought of not having a chance to speak with him. After all, he was a very important client for OSD and it was part of her job to welcome everyone and ensure his or her comfort. Regardless of the fact that Hunt was the only man to interest her since Brad had dumped her, he was off limits.

Period.

Her office door beckoned like a welcome oasis. With a sigh she stepped into the quiet room. Only a small Tiffany reading lamp in the far corner relieved the darkness. As she walked toward her desk, the tension left her body, especially her shoulders. She leaned against her desk to kick off one shoe.

"Don't do that."

A low, rough voice sounded from behind her. She froze when she recognized the voice as belonging to the man who'd haunted her thoughts for the past few hours. William Hunter.

"Put your shoe back on," he commanded.

She hooked her shoe with her toe and slid it back on. Secure on two feet again, she felt more in control. "Good evening, Hunt." Her voice wobbled and her throat felt dry. "What can I do for you?"

"And a good evening to you, Victoria." His voice was soft and low as he moved closer. "I think you know exactly what I want from you."

She shivered as he placed his hands on her shoulders. The heat of his palms seared her skin through the material of her jacket. She glanced at the darkened window to the left and all she could see was their silhouettes close together and his head bending down toward her.

"You wore it." His voice was husky.

She swallowed hard. "Yes." Her voice gave an odd little quiver that was very unlike her normal, businesslike tone. "I did."

His hands began a slow slide down her back. Her breath caught as he reached her waist. "I like knowing my gift rests against your skin, against your breasts." His voice dropped and his breath stirred the soft tendrils of hair that had escaped from her chignon. "Cupping your pussy."

She shuddered at the sound of raw lust in his voice. Her vagina clenched as liquid heat flooded it. It had been so long...so long...

His hands moved to the front of her jacket to loosen the buttons. Against her back, his heat and arousal were unmistakable. Her hips jerked and she had to restrain herself from grinding against that delicious hardness.

Her jacket gaped as his hands slid inside. Strong fingers moved against the silk of her camisole as her breath halted in her throat. Every inch of her body strained for his questing fingers, wanting his touch against her bare flesh. Her breath escaped in a whoosh as his thumb brushed her skin before his entire hand slipped under her camisole.

"Why did you send the lingerie?" She felt as if she would fly apart within seconds if something didn't take her mind off his hand inching ever higher. Already she was wet and ready and he'd barely touched her.

"The moment I laid eyes on you, I knew I had to have you." He reached her bra and released the front clasp with a practiced twist of his fingers. He removed the garment and allowed it to drop to the floor. He cupped her breast, palming her as if to judge her weight and size. He brushed his thumb over her aching peak and she purred.

He's a client.

He rolled her aroused nipple between his fingers and a whimper passed her lips. She pressed back. His erection was hard and throbbing against the crease of her buttocks. He had magic hands and she wanted so much more than the teasing touches he offered. She started to turn, but he stopped her by placing his hands on her shoulders.

"That isn't how this game will be played." He adjusted her toward the desk and away from him before he released her. "Face forward until I tell you it's all right to move."

Victoria started to object, but he gently hushed her as he skimmed the jacket off her shoulders and tossed it over her chair. She shivered as cool air chilled her overheated skin. She was intrigued. It had been a long time since anyone had presumed to tell her what to do and never had it been like this.

Strong fingers curled around each wrist as he guided her hands to the desk, forcing her to lean over the aged walnut. Her thighs pressed against the wood as his lips brushed her shoulder. He hooked her fingers over the edges, showing her how he wanted her to grip the desk. "Don't move, Victoria. Not until I allow it."

She was shocked by his command and even more surprised by the rush of arousal that followed. There was a telltale pulse beating between her legs and her sex felt warm and liquid. She hadn't been this aroused since Brad had tied her to his bed, given her a gentle spanking and then left her for over an hour to await his pleasure. But that was in the privacy of his apartment and behind closed, locked doors, not in her office, for crying out loud.

What the devil is happening to me?

Her grip tightened. Anyone could walk into her office and see her half-naked and pressed against her desk. Her reputation as well as her career hung in the balance and that wasn't something to toy with. She had to stop this madness before it went any further.

But all objections flew from her mind as he kissed the very tip of her spine. Shivers raced across her skin as he worked his way down her back, pressing kisses here and nipping her skin there through the camisole. His hands continued a slow, sensual massage as he reached the waist of her skirt. "Remove your camisole, Victoria."

She bit her lip. "I…"

"Remove it now." He stood. "You may take your hands from the desk to do so."

With trembling hands, she took hold of the hem and pulled the garment over her head. Her nipples beaded as the cool, air-conditioned air kissed them.

"You should never wear a bra. You have magnificent breasts." His hands skimmed her sides to caress the tender underside of her breasts.

"They're too big so I have to wear one." She quivered as his fingers touched her nipples.

"Nonsense, they're perfection. I forbid you to wear a bra or panties any time you're with me," he said.

Her vagina flooded with moisture at his command and she almost wept at the sheer perfection of the moment. Here was a Master the likes of which Brad could never be. Here was the man who could master her, teach her about the dark eroticism she so craved while taking her to the heights of pleasure.

But he was a client.

She closed her eyes as he continued his sensual assault on her breasts, leaving no inch untouched. Under normal circumstances, she'd say Hunt wasn't her type. He was a bad boy who'd been disinherited from his wealthy family while in his late teens. More at home in blue jeans than any man ought to be, he was a self-educated man. After he'd inherited the small, almost-bankrupt shipping company from a distant relative, he'd managed to build a multi-million dollar company from next to nothing.

His hands were large and calloused, and his feet were big. She wiggled her hips against his erection. Everything about Hunt was larger than life. She shivered in anticipation.

"Unzip your skirt."

She hesitated, knowing she should stop, but every cell in her body urged her to continue on the sensual journey he'd begun.

"Now, Victoria."

Her logical mind wanted to rebel against his command, but her innate desire to serve her Master won the inner struggle. She grasped the waist of her skirt and slid down the zipper. She pushed the soft material over her hips and carefully stepped out before tossing it over the back of her chair. Clad only in the thong panties, thigh highs and her heels, she felt as if she were having an out-of-body experience. Did he intend for her to display herself or was he going to take her here on her desk?

His breathing was harsh in her ear as he skimmed his hand over her buttocks and gave them a friendly squeeze. Sliding his hand between her thighs, he cupped her mons. She whimpered and thrust against his big hand, helpless to stop herself.

"Remove your panties."

With trembling hands, she slid them down and stepped away. She picked them up and started to toss them onto the chair with her other clothes.

"Hand them to me."

She crumpled the silk in her hand and she could feel the crotch was damp with her arousal. She hesitated, her cheeks flushed. "I—"

"Now, Victoria." Hunt took the garment from her limp hand and held them in front of her eyes, fingering the damp spot. "You creamed your panties, didn't you?" He raised them to within an inch of her nose and she inhaled her rich and loamy scent"You're very aroused, aren't you, Victoria?"

She couldn't answer, too ashamed to admit to the evidence that was literally staring her in the face. He leaned over her shoulder and raised the panties to his nose. His teeth met with a click and his grip on her waist tightened. Against her buttocks, she felt his cock straining against his pants.

"Oh yes, quite aroused." She was pleased to note the strained tone of his voice. "This is turning you on, standing before me naked like this."

"No," she mumbled.

"Liar." He tossed the panties onto the chair and stepped away. Victoria felt chilled without his big body covering her. "I won't tolerate liars and you'll do well to learn that."

Her heart raced. "W-w-what are you going to do?'

"I think you need a lesson. I'll teach you to never lie to me again. Now put your hands back on the desk the way I showed you."

She hesitated.

"Do it or your punishment will be worse."

Victoria swallowed and placed her hands on the desk, gripping the edge like she was told. From her position with her hips tilted backwards, she was exposed, helpless to stop him from doing anything he wanted to do. A thrill of naughtiness ran through her.

"Close your eyes, Victoria."

"I c-c-can't see you as you're behind me—"

"Do it now or I'll blindfold you. Would you like that, Victoria? To be blindfolded?" She heard the sound of him unbuckling his belt. "Or maybe you need a little corporal punishment to see the error of your ways?"

"No!" She was ashamed to realize that a part of her was extremely excited by the idea. Heavens above, was this really happening to her? Any minute now, she was going to wake up and find out that she'd fallen asleep in her office chair and was going to be late to the party. Her cunt flexed as Hunt brushed her buttocks with his leather belt.

"You're lying to me again, Victoria."

"N-n-no...I-I..." She squeezed her eyes shut. Any minute now, he was going to strike her...

She heard the buckle hit the desk as his hands gripped her hips, pushing her forward slightly. "Spread your legs and show yourself to me."

Biting her lip, she spread her legs as tension built in her body. When was the last time she'd been aroused like this? With Brad? Before him? Never? She fought the urge to grind her pussy against the desk and bring herself the relief she needed.

"I can see how hot and wet you are for me. You're enjoying this, aren't you?"

She remained silent.

"I'd recommend that you answer me." The soft leather pressed into the crack of her buttocks. "You enjoy exposing yourself? I see the evidence here between your thighs."

"Yes," she mumbled.

"Master."

"Yes, M-M-Master."

"Very good, Victoria." He removed the belt. "You learn quickly, though I'm not sure what to do with you at this point. You lied to me and that demands swift correction. However, as you're somewhat new to this game and obviously poorly trained, I think I'll be lenient. This time." He cupped her buttocks and gave them a squeeze. "Tonight, I have no desire to see your beautiful ass pinkened from the kiss of my belt, though I do think it would be a glorious sight to see."

She felt him slide a hand around her body and between her thighs. One thick finger parted her lips and entered her wet channel, eliciting a whimper. "I have other things in mind for you this evening." He removed his finger with a wet sound as her aroused flesh reluctantly released him. "Wait here. I'll be right back."

Alarmed, she straightened, forcing her wobbly knees to lock. "Where are you going?"

"It isn't your place to question me, woman. I'm the Master and I make all the rules. If I find that you've moved while I'm gone, I won't be lenient again." She heard the click of the bathroom door and soon the sound of running water.

Victoria opened her eyes. In a few seconds, she could grab her clothes and be back at the party before anyone even noticed she'd been gone. But a twinge between her thighs protested that thought. She was in need of a man to ease the ache. Of course, her right hand would do the trick. She wasn't sure, though, that she wanted Hunt to walk back into the room and catch her masturbating.

"Very good, Victoria. You learn quickly."

She started, mentally kicking herself for not hearing him return.

"You weren't thinking of leaving me, were you?"

"No."

"I think you're lying again." His breath was hot on her shoulder. "I think you were trying to figure out how long I'd be in the bathroom and if you could safely get away."

"Maybe—"

"Or you were thinking about what would happen if someone were to come into your office right now and see you spread across your desk like this." He slid his finger between her thighs and caressed her clitoris.

"Ahhh." Her hips followed his teasing movement.

"You were thinking about how they'd be shocked to see the proper Victoria Brittain sans clothing and arrayed in such a provocative fashion. Or maybe they'd touch you to see how hot you felt. And if you were lucky, they'd fill you with their cock and take you from behind." He removed his hand. "You need to come, don't you, Victoria?"

Her body shook with unrealized release. "Yes," she whispered.

"Yes, Master."

"Yes, Master," she parroted.

"Close your eyes and keep them closed this time."

She heard the soft hiss of a zipper being undone, then the sound of foil tearing. A condom?

"Now, Victoria." His voice was a liquid caress and she felt the tip of his cock press against the entrance of her sex. "What do you want me to do?"

"Enter me," she whispered.

"Master," he prompted.

"Enter me, Master."

She started as he grabbed her hips and thrust into her from behind. He was massive, and he pressed into her again and again until she'd taken him to the hilt. She reveled in the sensation of being filled, really filled this time. She clenched down, her inner muscles urging him to move.

"Now, what do you want?" He stood completely still inside of her. "Do your nipples hurt?" He slid his hands around her back to palm her breasts. "Do you want me to touch them?"

"Yes, Master."

He rubbed her erect nipples, sensitizing them, teasing until she squirmed under his touch. She moaned as he stopped and spanked her hard across the bottom. "I didn't say you could move, Victoria."

Victoria swallowed as tears stung her eyes. Here she was, over her desk and being penetrated by the biggest cock she'd ever felt and he wouldn't let her move. It was sheer torture. She ought to tell him where to get off. She could go downstairs to the party and pick almost any man, married or no, and they'd gladly fuck her until she could take no more.

"Much better." He dropped a kiss to her shoulder. "You're an apt student and you're learning your lessons well this evening. I shall have to reward you."

He trailed his hand down her abdomen and cupped her mons. He parted her labia and zeroed in on her clitoris. He began to rub the small nubbin and she struggled to not move, choosing to bite her lip instead. Behind her, he began to thrust.

She bit down harder, swallowing the cries that threatened to spill forth as he continued his sensual assault. She flexed against him, savoring the delicious sensation of his big cock pushing in and out of her wet channel as his finger stroked and teased. She tried to keep her body still, but as Hunt's thrusts grew more frantic, she couldn't help but push back to meet him.

The sound of her buttocks slapping his groin sounded loud in the still of the office. The familiar sensation of orgasm began in her calves, then slid up her legs, an intense sensation which increased in strength as it reached her groin before exploding with such force that it bent her double. She collapsed face first onto the desk as she felt Hunt's cock twitch as he moaned his pleasure and collapsed over her.

For a few moments they remained still, the upper halves of their bodies leaning heavily on the desk. Then he stood and withdrew himself. She heard him pulling his clothes back in place and she forced herself to rise.

"Get dressed," he ordered.

Silent, her mind spun with the ramifications of what had just taken place. Slowly she pulled her clothes on. Dressed again, she turned to face him.

Hunt stood near the window dressed in his tuxedo. His expression was remote, but his eyes were dark with satisfaction as he looked at her. Inside, she shivered.

"Do you have plans this weekend?" he asked.

She shook her head. Other than catching up on some reading, she hadn't made any plans at all.

"I'll send a car for you in the morning." He withdrew a business card from his jacket and laid it on the desk. "You'll need toiletries and business attire for your return to work on Monday."

"But—"

"That's all you'll need."

For a second she wanted to refuse, but Victoria had the vague feeling that would be a big mistake. Hunt held the keys to a world she wanted to explore. Brad had given her a taste of decadence while Hunt was offering her a full sensual banquet. Now she needed to muster the courage to reach out and take it. Silent, she nodded.

"Until tomorrow, then." Hunt exited her office, closing the door behind him.

Victoria sank into one of the desk chairs and closed her eyes. The man was powerful, and sex with him had been earth shattering. She licked her lips. Had she just agreed to spend the weekend with him? She moaned. Hunt was a client. What in the devil's name did she think she was doing by jeopardizing their professional relationship?

She opened her eyes and picked up his business card. It was white with blue lettering, his name, office address and contact numbers. In handwritten bold script was his cell phone number. Did she go with him or decline his offer? There was still time to turn him down. Her cunt gave a twinge at the thought of never indulging in the sensual excess he offered.

When was the last time she'd done something rash just for herself? Especially something as deliciously wicked as this? Hunt held the keys to the world she'd longed to discover; would she regret it later if she declined his offer because she was scared?

She dropped the card on the desk. No, she would go and, for the first time in her life, Victoria dared to damn the consequences of her actions.

Chapter Three

Hunt released a sigh of relief as the limo cleared the tree-lined drive and came into view. Victoria had arrived. Even though she'd agreed to join him last night, he wasn't sure she'd follow through with it. Ever since he'd left her, he'd kept his cell phone close at hand just in case she caved and told him she'd changed her mind.

It took all his willpower to keep from pressing his nose against the window as the dark blue car stopped near the front door. He'd been planning this weekend in his mind for over a year. Ever since he'd met the beautiful advertising exec, he'd known he had to have her. Finding out from Brad, her miserable ex-fiancé, that Victoria had been into "kink", as he called it, had been an added bonus. Not that Hunt considered bondage and discipline to be kink. To him, it was a way of life.

The black-suited driver exited the car and moved around to open her door. One slim, stocking-clad leg emerged, followed by the woman who'd haunted his dreams.

She'd dressed conservatively for the hour-long drive. A full black skirt fell to mid-shin and a short-sleeved gray sweater and black leather boots completed her outfit. Why a woman this beautiful chose to dress so plainly was beyond him. This wasn't the outfit a woman wore to meet her lover. This was what she'd wear to meet with her tax attorney. Her soft brown hair was pulled back into a tidy twist and a pair of sunglasses concealed her expressive eyes. His groin tightened at the thought of looking into those bewitching eyes of hers as he brought her to completion.

Victoria smiled in appreciation as she accepted a small bag from the driver. Her toiletries and a single outfit of work clothes no doubt. He was pleased to see that she'd followed his directions and left her clothing behind. As the driver shut the door, she glanced about her. He wondered what she thought of his massive Tudor home with its immaculate manicured lawn. She ran a nervous hand over her smooth coil of hair before the driver ushered her to the front door and out of his sight.

Hunt stepped away from the window. The next twelve hours would be eye opening for the lovely Victoria. He had no doubt that Brad was a bumbling Dom and Victoria's slight education had probably left her unfulfilled at best. Hunt was about to reintroduce her to a world she was born to inhabit.

He picked up a purple latex tickler from his desk. The smooth handle was approximately four inches long and dangling from one end were several hundred thin latex strands. He shook the tickler against his palm and the feeling was subtle and soothing. Raising it, he cracked the toy against his bare arm, enjoying the rush of pleasure/pain that shot through his nervous system.

He'd seen a tickler wielded by a Master bring a properly trained sexual slave to orgasm in minutes. He'd also seen an inept Master scar a sub with a cane. In his world, there was an equal balance of danger as well as pleasure to be enjoyed.

He ran his fingers through the soft latex strands. There were many other toys he could use, but the tickler was one of his personal favorites and he could hardly wait to experience Victoria's reaction. He dropped it into an open desk drawer, anticipation running high in his system as he hastened to greet his guest.

* * * * *

Victoria stood in the middle of the sumptuously appointed bedroom, her hands clenching and unclenching by her side. Her heart thudded in her chest as she stared out the French doors overlooking the back gardens.

What am I doing here?

The brilliant sunshine was blinding and she stared at the deep green grass without even seeing it. Even as she'd dressed this morning, she'd battled with her decision to venture to Hunt's home. She wasn't the type to indulge in a careless fling and that's exactly what this was, a fling, and with a client no less. Her life had always been about order—order and making the right choices. Her mother had died when Victoria was only eleven years old and her father had been consumed with making a living for her and her brothers.

Even at a young age, her brothers had turned to her for emotional stability and support. Even though she wasn't the eldest, she'd become the responsible one. The one who'd made sure dinner was on the table, laundry was done and the bills were paid on time. It had all been left to her. Even in high school, when the other kids were behaving badly in the backseats of their parent's cars, she'd been home tutoring her youngest brother in algebra. She'd never been allowed to be irresponsible. Maybe that's why she was here today. After last night's heady exchange of power, she hungered for more.

Much more.

"Victoria, welcome to my home."

Hunt came into the bedroom and for a second her breath caught in her throat. Whereas the room was all lightness, Hunt was the exact opposite. Dressed in black jeans and a matching T-shirt, he was the complete absence of color. His dark hair was combed back from his handsome face and his smile was wide and welcoming.

"Thank you. You have a very beautiful home."

He took her hands in his and pressed a chaste kiss to her cheek. His scent, a mixture of cinnamon and warm male skin, caused her toes to curl in her leather boots.

"Did you have a pleasant trip?" He released her hands.

"Very."

"Excellent. Let's sit down to some lunch and we can talk." He walked to the closet and opened the door. "Your clothing is in here. Pick one and I'll meet you at the base of the steps. We're dining on the back terrace."

"Sounds lovely."

"I'm very glad you're here, Victoria." His dark gaze seemed to penetrate her clothing and caress her skin.

Her throat dry, she gave him a weak smile. "Thanks…" Her voice cracked and she cleared her throat. "Thanks for inviting me."

"You're welcome." He exited, then turned to look at her through the open door, his hand on the knob. "Victoria, don't keep me waiting." The door shut with a quiet snick and she sprang into action.

In the large closet hung a line of summer shifts. She selected one in the palest of blue. Stripping out of her clothes, she donned the shift, dismayed to see that not only was it at least eight inches shorter than anything she was accustomed to wearing, the back was low-cut and she would be unable to wear her bra. Of course, Hunt had told her not to wear any lingerie around him but she'd feel naked and vulnerable without them. Reluctantly she removed the lace and underwire garment and tossed it on the bed.

Opting to leave her panties in place, for now at least, she eyed herself in the mirror. The color was flattering and the hem skimmed her thigh-high stockings so they could at least stay and she wouldn't feel quite so bare. But it was just so…flimsy. It was rare when she went out in public with most of her shoulders and back bare. She twisted around, making sure everything was in its place and all essentials were covered. After selecting a pair of sandals, she was ready to go for lunch.

The hall was empty as she slipped from her room and she passed several closed doors before she reached the stairs. Hunt stood at the bottom of the steps, his gaze fixed on his watch and a slight frown marring his face. Her palms felt moist as she hastened down the steps, trying not to stumble, when his head came up and his gazed moved over her scanty attire.

"I thought I was going to have to fetch you." He said, his tone deceptively lazy.

"No." Her voice was breathless. "Just ironing out a slight zipper issue."

He smiled and took her hand and she hoped he didn't notice her trembling. Tucking her fingers into the crook of his arm, he led her through the house and outside to the back terrace. A massive oak tree shaded one end and beneath it was a table set for two. A young woman was setting covered plates on the table.

"Thank you, Nan. It looks good." Hunt said.

She beamed at the compliment. "Is there anything else I can get for you, sir?"

"Not right now, thank you."

The woman gave Victoria a shy smile as she left.

He drew a chair out and ushered her into it. After seating her, he dropped a soft kiss on the exposed skin of her shoulder. "You look lovely in this dress, Victoria."

She shivered, detecting the heated dark tones of desire in his voice. "Thank you, it's beautiful, though it doesn't cover much." She tugged the hem into place.

"Which is exactly why I enjoy the view so much." Hunt gave her a careless smile as he whisked the dome away from her plate.

She blushed and dropped her gaze to the organic salad with raspberry vinaigrette dressing. Picking up her fork, she focused her attention on her food, trying to ignore the handsome man sitting a few feet away. After she'd devoured half her salad, he broke their silence.

"Did you spend the last twelve hours trying to decide how to gracefully decline my invitation?"

Her fork hit the plate with a loud clang. Carefully setting it aside, she looked at him. "What makes you think that?"

He chuckled. "I know you, Victoria. You probably spent most of the night worrying over your decision like a dog with a bone."

Stung, she shot back, "I'm not sure that I like that analogy."

Hunt sat back as a young man in dark trousers and a pristine white shirt appeared to take their salad plates away. "I'm well aware that what happened last night was probably a first. It is common for a first-timer to be nervous and more than a little apprehensive about indulging themselves as we did. To give up all of your power, your very breath, to someone else is a heady yet frightening experience."

Mortified, Victoria darted a look at the young man's impassive face. He gave no hint that he listened as he served their lunch. Without a word, he placed their plates on the table and gave them a sketchy bow before leaving.

"Did you have to say that in *front* of him?" she hissed.

Unperturbed, Hunt picked up his fork. "I pay my employees well to complete their tasks efficiently. Kent is paid to do his job, not speculate upon what I do in the privacy of my own bedroom." He gestured to her plate. "Eat before it gets cold."

She picked up the fork and took a bite of the poached salmon. The more she chewed, the more the morsel seemed to expand. Just as she feared she'd choke, she forced herself to swallow.

"Why me?" She set down her fork. "Why did you choose me?"

His brow rose. "Because you're the perfect submissive." He gestured for her to eat again. "Or at least you will be once I've properly trained you."

"B-but what if I don't want to be a s-s-submissive?" She picked at the fish, using it as an excuse to avoid his knowing gaze.

"Look. I know you've had a taste of your own power before now. You're also a textbook example of the perfect sub. You work in a position of power and you've had to be responsible all your life. You practically raised your brothers even though you're younger than all but one and you did so from a very young age. No one has ever shown the desire to take care of you." He leaned forward, his eyes glowing with excitement. "Don't you want to be able to hand that responsibility to someone else? To have someone make the decisions for you for a change? You'd be a living vessel of pleasure, given and received. Your every need would be met and you'd want for nothing."

She bit her lip. The picture he painted was attractive. It would be lovely, for a while anyway, to not have to make all the decisions. To only have to concentrate on pleasuring herself and her lover. And to let someone else shoulder the burdens of her hectic life for a while, even if only for a few hours.

Her gaze met his darker one. "What would I have to do?"

"Whatever I tell you."

Alarmed, she dropped the fork. "And what if I don't want to do whatever you say?"

"We'll have a safe word. A word you can use to tell me you're not enjoying what we're doing. Whenever you feel uncomfortable, just say the word and we'll back off. How does that sound?"

Victoria nodded slowly as Kent approached with dessert. She glanced down; surprised to see her plate was almost empty.

"What do you want your safe word to be?" Hunt asked.

Her gaze caught on the dessert, a small dish of pale fruity sherbet. "Orange."

Kent set a bowl in front of each of them and backed away as silently as he'd arrived.

"Are you ready to begin your lessons, Victoria?"

She swallowed audibly, her gaze clashing with his. She wasn't sure what she wanted. She knew she wanted this man to fuck her again. She knew that last night had been an experience like none other in her life and he was offering her the heady chance to experience more. To teach her to know her own body, her own limitations. To explore the dark side of her sexuality, the part of her that Brad had barely begun to touch.

Almost against her will, she nodded and she didn't miss the spark of triumph in his eyes.

"Good. Now get up."

Her heart in her throat, she hesitated. What was he going to ask her to do?

"Victoria," his tone was chiding. "Remember, you have to obey me. You can use your safe word only if you're feeling threatened or uncomfortable. So either use it or get on your feet. Now."

Silent, she rose and pushed her chair under the table.

"Now, come to me."

On shaky knees, she approached him. As she neared, he pushed away from the small table.

"Remove your panties and hand them to me."

Her eyes widened and again she hesitated.

"Victoria, don't make me tell you again. If you do, I'll have to punish you." His voice was matter of fact. "I told you last night, no undergarments when you're with me. I want you completely accessible."

She swallowed hard and, with shaking hands, skimmed her panties down her legs. The soft breeze tickled her bare skin before her skirt fell back into place. She handed the garment to him. Her cunt clenched as he raised it to his nose and inhaled.

"If I could bottle this scent…"

She blushed.

"Now, spread your legs and sit in my lap."

This time she didn't hesitate. She lowered herself onto his thighs and his jeans were faintly rough against her bare buttocks. His big hands came to rest on her lower thighs before they slid beneath her skirt.

"While you're here in my home, you're forbidden to wear undergarments of any kind. You'll eat when you're hungry, and you'll sleep beside me in my bed." He skimmed his fingers over her hip. "You're here for my pleasure and my pleasure alone, unless I request otherwise." His knuckles brushed the generous underside of her left breast. "In giving me pleasure, you'll receive pleasure. Is this understood?"

Victoria gasped as he tweaked her erect nipple and she nodded.

"Yes, Master," he prompted.

"Y-y-yes, Master."

"You have a beautiful body, one that's made for giving and receiving pleasure. We're going to explore your sexuality like you never have before." He slipped his hand from under her dress and released her. "Now, get on your knees and suck me off."

She started to object before she caught the gleam of anticipation in his eyes. He wanted her to object. He was waiting for the opportunity to correct her behavior. She ducked her head and slid from his lap to kneel on the sun-warmed stones of the terrace. His impressive erection strained against the placket of his jeans. Shoving any misgivings aside, she undid the button and lowered the zip to reveal strained black silk boxers.

"Lower the bodice of your dress. I want to see your breasts as you take me into your mouth."

Eyes down, she slid the straps of her dress from her shoulders, allowing the top to slide to her waist. The soft breeze caressed her sensitive flesh and she shivered as she reached for his cock. She opened the silk placket and his hardened flesh sprang free.

There was no doubt about it. Hunt was a big, big man.

With the sun warm on her exposed skin, she took the broad head of his cock into her mouth. He tasted of the sea and warm potent male as she dragged her tongue over the tip, relishing his unique flavor. How long had it been since she'd had a man in her mouth? Brad had never been big on oral sex, either giving or receiving, and she'd missed this particularly intimacy. Hunt's hips gave an involuntary twitch as she rubbed her thumb along the sensitive underside of his delicious cock.

"You have the most beautiful breasts I've ever seen." His voice was strained. "You have no idea what the sight of you, between my knees and my cock buried in your talented lips, does to me."

Oh, but she did.

The rush of feminine power surged through her body. He might command her to do as he wished, but even as his sub she could bring him to his knees. She had him in her mouth, right where she wanted him.

Not missing a stroke, she reached for a bottle of olive oil on the table. As she poured a small amount into her palm, their gazes met and his was dark with heated approval. His breath caught as she wrapped her hand around him and moved in long, bold strokes as she worked his hardened flesh with her hand and mouth.

"Victoria, my god."

His fingers tangled in her hair, loosening the soft twist at the back of her head as she closed her eyes, concentrating her entire being on fucking him with her mouth. He tried to control her movements, but she resisted, wanting to keep him at her mercy. Against her body, she could feel the tension in his thighs. He was close now, very close.

She swirled her tongue around his sensitive head, tasting the ambrosia of pre-cum and rich olive oil. She increased her movements; her hand stroked his thick root as she took him deep into her throat. His hips arched and his thighs jerked as he climaxed into her mouth with an anguished groan.

Victoria let his cock slip from her lips and rested her cheek against his thigh. His breathing was rough as if he'd just run a marathon.

"You have the mouth of a virtuoso," he said.

She grinned. "And you have a cock well-worthy of my talents."

"Flatterer." He ruffled her hair gently. "Now, get up. We're not through yet."

A quiver of excitement snaked through her belly as she rose to her feet. Feeling like a slattern with her breasts bared to the warm sun and his even hotter gaze, she fought the urge to cover herself.

"Perfect." He tweaked one erect nipple with his thumb and forefinger. He took care to reassemble his clothing before he cleared his end of the table. "Sit here." He patted the tabletop.

Nervous yet excited, Victoria sat on the table, her knees primly held together. Hunt gave her a small smile as he pulled his chair closer and he sat, parting her thighs with his chest. Her vagina clenched as he reached for the dessert bowl of half-melted sherbet.

He urged her to scoot to the edge of the table, her heels balanced on the armrests of his chair, and then his calloused fingers opened her. The sherbet was cool against her heated skin as he painted her pussy with the sweet liquid. At the first touch of his tongue, Victoria let loose a scream that would have embarrassed her under normal circumstances. Now, the only thing that mattered was each swipe of his magical tongue.

She tilted her head back, her hips settling into a complementary rhythm as his tongue teased and aroused. His fingers drove hard and deep into her dripping cunt until she cried out, her hips jerking wildly with each thrust. With a brush of his thumb, she came against his mouth, her screams thrown up to the sunlit sky.

Dizzy with completion, Victoria realized she was truly his captive now.

Chapter Four

"But what if I don't want to be tied up?"

Hunt heard the note of unease in her voice. Training Victoria to be his submissive would be hard work, but once she overcame her knee-jerk conservative reactions, she would come to enjoy it, nay, crave it, as much as he did.

"I know you're a little apprehensive." He tucked her hand into the crook of his arm as they walked along the shadowy path of the garden. They'd just eaten a leisurely dinner and now he was preparing to take her into his bed. "A little fear will add spice to your excitement, I promise you. I'll never do anything that would cause too much pain and you can call a halt to our activities at any time. Just remember your safety word when you feel the need."

She bit her lip and didn't say anything. He wanted to chuckle at the mix of confusion and yearning he saw on her face. "Have you ever had anal sex?"

She shook her head. "No, never."

"Why not?"

"It looks painful."

Hunt turned a corner and began steering her back toward the house. "If it's done improperly and without careful preparation, it can be very painful.

We've known each other for several years now and we both trust each other. You hold the financial future of my company in your hands and I hold a great deal of income for OSD in mine. You know I'd never hurt you, right?"

She nodded.

"Okay then." He opened the door and ushered her inside. "We'll go slowly, one step at a time. We're in no hurry at all."

Upstairs in his bedroom, he directed her to strip off her dress. He was pleased to see that she'd obeyed his command and hadn't worn any undergarments. Her skin was kissed by the sunshine from their afternoon romp and she fairly glowed with good health. Her palm was cool as he took her hand in his and led her to the foot of the bed. Earlier he'd suspended a thick chain from the ceiling that ended with a round ring at just the right height for her to grip with both hands. He showed her how to wrap her fingers around the dangling ring.

"Relax your back."

He skimmed his palms down her body until she calmed beneath his touch and was close to purring. He knew her nudity was giving her cause for consternation, especially since he was still fully clothed. When would women realize that the naked form was beautiful and not something to be hidden beneath layers?

"When we come here, unless I instruct you otherwise, you're to assume this position." He moved around her to sit on the small bench at the foot of the bed. "Are you comfortable?"

"Yes, Master."

"Good." He rose and shed his shirt, strolling across the room to pour himself a brandy. He was all too aware of the beautiful woman who watched him with liquid brown eyes. He set his glass on the bedside table and removed the rest of his clothes. When he was naked, he climbed onto the bed.

She was a glorious sight. Her expression was a mixture of arousal and unease. The light from a single lamp near the bed illuminated her luscious curves. Her ample breasts were pale, her nipples big and broad and the soft color of peaches. He'd always been a breast man and he could hardly wait to fuck them. At that provocative thought, his cock hardened. Oh, how good all that warm flesh would feel wrapped around his member.

Her waist was slim and her hips flared out nicely. Just the right proportion for a man to hang onto. Between her legs was a neat thatch of dark curls; soft and pretty like the rest of her. Her long legs were sturdy and nicely curved, her feet slimly arched and her toenails were polished pale pink. All in all, Victoria Brittain was one lovely woman.

"Come to me."

She released her grip on the ring and walked closer. Her hips and breasts swayed with each step. The bed dipped as she climbed onto it.

"Take me in your mouth."

Her dark eyes flashed as she climbed between his splayed thighs. She sat back on her heels and studied his burgeoning erection as if she were contemplating the lunch menu at her favorite restaurant.

"Do it now or I'll spank you…"

Her gaze on his cock, she leaned forward and sucked him into her mouth. He grit his teeth as her talented tongue swirled along the head, immediately zeroing in on the sensitive underside. She laved his cock with her tongue, leaving no part of him untouched. One hand curled around the base of his shaft while her other hand cradled his balls. He moaned as she gently cupped his sac, undulating her hand around his cock. If she kept this up, the game would be over all too soon.

"Turn around. I want your pussy where I can reach it."

He smothered a chuckle at how quickly she obeyed. Without interrupting her assault on his body, she turned so she straddled his chest. He could see that she was wet, very wet, already.

Good, that was what he wanted.

His fingers parted her labia and she twitched beneath his touch and arched her back, pushing her cunt toward his face. He found her clit and sucked on it, enjoying the taste that was uniquely hers. His tongue seduced while his hands caressed her lush backside. His tongue licked her clit slowly as her hips thrust against his face, burying him in damp womanly flesh. He grabbed her hips, holding her in place as he brought her to completion with his tongue. She released him from her mouth and screamed, her body shaking in reaction.

As her body sank across him, he reached beneath his pillow and removed a small leather case he'd placed there earlier. Inside the case was an anal plug, the smallest he could find, and a generous tube of lubricant. Her breathing was ragged as he parted her cheeks and inserted the tube. She stiffened as the cool gel flooded her anus.

"It's just lubricant, Victoria." He spread the gel with his finger, making sure her anus was well greased. "It's very important to use a generous amount if I don't want to hurt you." He entered her with one finger and she stiffened, her head coming up from his thighs. "Now, relax." He squirted more lubricant into her anus before testing her again, this time judging her to be ready.

With one hand he stroked her back while he picked up the small, dark purple plug with the other. Spreading her cheeks, he pressed the plug against her tiny, round ring of muscle until it gave way and the plug was inserted. He smiled when she gave an experimental wriggle.

Hunt shifted her to his side, then cleaned his hands on a towel. He moved on the bed until they were face to face. "How does it feel?"

She wiggled again, concentrating on the sensation. "Full."

He smiled. "You'll get used to it, even look forward to it. After a period of time, we'll use bigger plugs until your body can accept my cock into your lovely ass." He slid his hand between her legs. "You're so wet for me. Have you always been this responsive?"

She shook her head. "Not always."

He felt a surge of triumph. He'd bet she'd never been this responsive to Brad. That was why they'd been such a bad pairing. Brad wasn't the Dom for her, but he was.

He rolled onto his back and pulled her on top of him. Spreading her legs, he eased into her damp channel, filling her, stretching her. He watched her face as the twin sensations of a full cunt and anus swamped her. He surged into her as her expression turned to one of total enchantment.

"How does it feel?"

She wiggled and he swallowed a groan. "Odd, but I like it."

Hunt chuckled and he reached around and gave the plug a gentle twist. She moaned; her eyes slid half closed. He adjusted his thrust and set the pace, driving in and out of her, his cock straining for completion. She was panting, her head thrashing about, her hair tangling on her shoulders as he fucked her.

A warning rush moved down his spine, signaling his impending climax. It was now or never. Reaching around her, he gave the plug another twist and she screamed. Her release moved through her like a tidal wave as it tipped him over the edge.

Her vagina was still contracting around him as she sank to his chest, her nipples pressed into him. He closed his eyes and felt her heart thundering against him.

She was… perfect.

The sun was already high in the sky as Victoria finished dressing. When was the last time she'd gotten out of bed after sunrise? She shook her head. She couldn't remember the last time she'd lazed in bed so long. When she'd awoken, Hunt was already up and gone, his side of the bed cool to her touch. She'd felt curiously abandoned until she'd seen the note in the bathroom telling her to get dressed and join him outside for a breakfast picnic.

Her hand hovered over the small selection of panties she'd tucked into her make-up case. Should she put on a pair? Surely he didn't expect her to picnic without panties. She cringed at the thought of sitting on the ground without some barrier of protection between her pussy and the grass. Her mind made up, she selected a pink pair and slid them on. It wasn't like she couldn't take them off again. Besides, what was he going to do? Spank her?

Maybe, just maybe…

After checking that her hair was neatly contained in a loose ponytail, she headed for the kitchen. The scent of baking bread and lemon cleaner hung in the air. Hunt lived in a very efficient household; that was for sure. Other than Nan the cook, there was Kent and a maid she'd yet to see. It must be nice to be one of the filthy rich.

As she entered the kitchen, she saw Hunt tuck a bottle of wine into a basket. He was chatting with Nan as she stirred a large pot on the stove. What was it about this man that had aroused her from the first moment she'd met him? It wasn't just his good looks, though that helped. Maybe it was the combination of his bad boy image and the aura of power he wore so carelessly. She'd seem him in action during marketing meetings. He was a man who knew what he wanted and wasn't afraid to reach out and grab it. And, for now, he wanted her. A shiver of awareness moved through her body.

As if sensing her presence, he turned. "There you are." He shot her a warm glance.

She gave him a shy smile then spoke to Nan. "Good morning."

"Morning, Miss Victoria. I trust you slept well?"

Victoria shot her a look but found only a smile, no hint of knowledge about anything that transpired behind closed doors. "I slept very well. Thank you for asking."

"Come." Hunt held out his hand. "I'm getting hungry and I'm sure you are as well."

"What are we having?" She took his hand, enjoying the sense of warmth and belonging that surrounded her at his touch. She fell into step beside him as he picked up the basket and they walked out the back door.

"You'll see." He gave her an enigmatic smile.

He led her down a garden path. Soon they left the manicured acres behind. The sun was warm overhead as they walked, talking about their lives and their respective companies. Swapping tales about their jobs, friends and common interests. Several times she laughed out loud as he shared some of his more interesting exploits abroad.

They rounded a small group of trees and he led her to a grassy area beneath a large towering tree. "This is the spot."

"Lovely." She took the blanket he offered and spread it across the soft grass, bending to straighten a corner.

"Victoria."

She straightened, startled by his suddenly cool tone. "Yes?"

"Are you wearing panties?" He set down the basket.

She gave a jerky nod. "I didn't know if I'd have to sit on the ground…"

"You've disappointed me." He crossed his muscular arms across his chest and she felt a trickle of unease race down her back. "You disobeyed my order and you didn't trust me enough to take care of you." He shook his head. "We discussed the rules and you've deliberately broken them." He stepped closer and took her hand, his fingers curling around her wrist. "You know what'll happen now, don't you?"

She swallowed hard and shook her head.

"Your actions are going to force me to punish you." He kissed the tender skin of her inner wrist. "Now, remove your panties and give them to me." He released her.

With trembling hands—from excitement or fear, she didn't want to guess—she took off the offending garment and handed it to him. Without even looking, he tucked it into his pants pocket. He then turned and walked a few feet away to where a thick, fallen trunk formed a small bench.

"Come to me."

On wobbly knees, she approached.

"You're scared, aren't you?" He shook his head. "You needn't be afraid. This won't be terribly painful as I'm going to use my hand rather than a belt. Your inability to obey your Master forced us to this place. Do you understand what I'm telling you?"

She nodded, unable to speak.

Hunt patted his lap. "Lay over my knees, face down. Don't worry, I won't drop you."

She lowered her body across his until her hands and feet were in the soft grass and her abdomen lay across his lap. Against her side, she could feel his arousal. He was enjoying this!

"Relax." He flipped up her skirt, exposing her backside to the bright sun. "When this is over, we can enjoy our meal."

His big hands stroked her skin, squeezing, caressing the globes of her buttocks. Though most of her body was still covered, she felt horribly exposed, the soft breeze was cool and the sun warm as he rubbed and stroked. She squirmed as the first trickles of arousal snaked through her cunt. He nibbled on one buttock; his lips warm as his teeth gently worried her flesh. He continued rubbing and stroking as he spread her legs, the warm air caressing her inner flesh.

Maybe this won't be so bad after all–

Then, without warning, he hit her.

She tensed. It had been a soft pat, no more than a parent would give a reluctant child. First on one cheek, then the other. With his second hand, he continued stroking even as the blows increased in number and strength. She struggled to get free as her buttocks warmed.

"Now, Victoria. Don't make me seriously punish you for resisting," he said. "Your ass is going to be a lovely shade of pink." He smacked her again and she stifled a groan. "If only I had a camera."

She squealed in protest and tried to rise, but he pushed her back down. "Relax, this will soon be over." The spanks and petting continued and tears stung her eyes. Would he never finish with her?

Slowly, the blows faded and she became aware of heat on her backside. Hunt rearranged her skirt before helping her to her feet.

"There now, all done." He pulled her into his arms and she leaned into him, burying her face in his shirt. "When we get back to the house, I have some arnica lotion that will soothe the sting."

He released her and returned to the blanket, leaving her confused and aroused at the same time. She watched as he sat and pulled items from the basket as if nothing had happened.

"Come," he said. "Eat. Nan prepared a wonderful feast."

Silent, she approached, then hesitated, unsure that she wanted to sit on her stinging behind.

He gave her an understanding look. "Just lay on your side. You'll be more comfortable and you can still eat." He waited until she stretched out, then handed her a small bunch of grapes. "Are you angry?"

She twirled the grapes, then set them on her plate. "No. I knew I was disobeying you when I put them on."

He picked up a slice of apple. "Then why did you do it?"

"I think a part of me wanted to see what you'd do." She looked away. "Now I'm confused."

"About?"

She shrugged, embarrassed to say that she was wet with arousal. What kind of person got off on being hit?

As if he could read her thoughts, he answered her. "Victoria, the skin is the largest organ of the body and also one of the most sensitive. What you're feeling right now is common for the early stages of your training. Your body enjoyed the stimulus while your mind tried to reject it." He picked a grape from her bunch and held it out to her. "You need to learn to quiet your mind and let your body dictate your actions."

She leaned forward and took the grape from his fingers with her mouth as she contemplated his words. It was hard to just throw away a lifetime of perceptions so quickly. She was also shocked to realize how aroused she was—her cunt was soaking wet and in desperate need of a firm touch to bring her off.

"Victoria, remove your dress."

She darted a glance at his face. His expression was cool and his eyes heated. Remembering the feel of his cock against her belly as he'd spanked her, she moved to her knees and shed the garment.

Hunt moved behind her and cupped her breasts, squeezing just enough to wring a whimper from her. Her hips moved restlessly as if they had a mind of their own. She needed release so badly. Would he allow her to have it?

"Spread your legs for me, Victoria."

Not needing another command, she spread her legs, almost sobbing as his hand slid over her slick flesh.

"See what I told you? Beautiful." His thick fingertips zeroed in on her erect clit. "You're so hot for me. You, my dear, are a true submissive in every sense of the word."

His words were all but drowned by her frantic cries as his fingers moved expertly over her aroused flesh. Her hips jerked with each movement as he brought her to an orgasm so strong she would have fallen face first if his arm hadn't been around her waist.

She was dimly aware of being lowered to the blanket, the material soft against her aroused skin. Then he stretched out beside her, his body spooning hers. Exhausted mentally and physically, she allowed her mind to shut down and she slipped into a light sleep.

Chapter Five

Nude with the exception of a blue silk thong, Victoria stood at attention in her practiced position at the foot of his bed. Her arms were stretched overhead and her hands clasped the metal ring. Behind her, she could hear Hunt shuffling items in a drawer.

After their late breakfast, they'd returned to the bedroom and he'd rubbed an almond-scented cream into her reddened buttocks and thighs. Surprisingly enough, the discomfort had faded almost immediately to a soft, warm glow.

She heard a drawer slide shut and the approach of heavy footsteps. Her shoulders were beginning to ache from remaining in such an awkward position.

Hunt gave her a gentle pat on her hip. "Perfect." He reached for her hands and lowered them. "Are you sore?"

She rotated her shoulders. "Just a little stiff."

"Don't worry, that'll soon fade as you grow more accustomed to the position." He produced a pair of leather handcuffs attached by a short chain and two spring clips. "Will you wear these for me?"

Her sex moistened at the sight of the cuffs and the scent of new leather. Suddenly shy, she nodded and held out her wrists, wanting to feel the caress of leather against her skin.

"And your safe word is?"

"Orange."

"Good." He opened a cuff and encircled one wrist. It fastened with a leather strap that slid through a metal loop. The inside was lined with padded silk and felt cool against her skin. She shivered as he attached the second one. "Cold?"

"Just a little."

He gave her a mysterious smile. "Don't worry, you'll be warm soon."

Taking the chain that held the cuffs together, he led her out of the room and down the hall. The carpet was thick beneath her bare feet as he led her to a door at the far end. He retrieved a key from the pocket of his jeans.

"Victoria, you must never reveal to anyone what you see in this room." He brushed a finger over her lower lip and she shivered. "Everything within is designed to heighten pleasure, not to cause pain." He smiled. "Well, not much anyway. Do you understand?"

She nodded, her throat tight. Part of her wanted to run as far and as fast as she could while another part, the larger part, wanted desperately to see what awaited them.

"That's my girl."

He opened the door and entered, pulling her behind him. The scent of musk, incense and leather teased her nose. Hunt flicked on a wall switch and muted lighting flooded the room. She could barely contain the gasp that forced its way into her throat.

The room was large with red walls and black carpeting. The windows were covered in thick, light-restricting drapes, giving the room a cocoon-like feel. Displayed along the walls were a variety of devices obviously meant for human restraint. A selection of whips, paddles, blindfolds and other devices she'd never seen before were suspended from a rack to the left. A padded massage table with leather restraints stood along the far wall. On the other side was something that looked like a padded sawhorse and next to it was a wrought iron cage large enough for an adult to stand inside.

In the center of the room, a sling was hung from the ceiling, its leather seat thankfully unoccupied. There were several brocade couches scattered about the various apparatuses in the room. No doubt for observers to watch in comfort. She'd never seen anything like this in her life.

Hunt shut the door and locked it. "Come, I have a new toy I wish to try out."

She was mute as he led her past a whipping post and an X frame. She'd never been bound to anything other than a bed and she was starting to feel a little nervous. He led her to a low, padded Y-shaped bench and he motioned for her to sit in the notch of the Y. She flinched as cool leather touched her sensitive backside.

Hunt dropped to his knees and skimmed his hands down her leg. Reaching her ankle, he raised her foot, nuzzling the arch.

"You're so beautiful, Victoria." He placed her leg on one of the branches of the Y and began buckling a leather restraint to her ankle. "More beautiful, more responsive than I'd even dreamed."

She shivered as he picked up her other leg and gave it the same treatment, binding her to the bench with her thighs splayed wide. Her cunt clenched as she felt the gentle brush of his fingertips over her mound. Her hips arched and he smiled in satisfaction.

"So responsive to me." He kissed the tender area just below her belly button, then urged her to lie back. Moving to her side, he reached underneath and pulled out two retractable pieces at shoulder height. He unhooked the spring clips on her wrists and attached them to the arm pieces. She was well and truly bound.

"Comfortable?" he asked.

She flexed her shoulders. "Yes, Master."

"Good, we shall begin." Hunt moved to a small table nearby. "From the first time I saw you, I imagined you here in this room with me." He selected an item from the table and returned to her side. "Lying here helpless, waiting for my pleasure and, in turn, your own."

He pulled a long black feather from behind his back. Running the feather up her arm, he swirled it over her breast until her nipple hardened. Then he drew it across every inch of her body, her skin tingling with every delicate swipe of the feather. Soon she was straining toward it.

"I want to talk about your fantasies, Victoria." He put the feather aside and picked up an artist's paintbrush. She almost swooned as the soft hairs traced her areola, narrowly missing the aroused tip. "What are your fantasies?"

"You fucking me," she gasped as the wicked tip dipped into her belly button.

He gave a pleased chuckle. "That will happen soon enough." He traced a circular hypnotic path up and down the inside of her thighs until she strained against her restraints. Was he trying to drive her mad?

"Tell me more of your fantasies."

Her mind whirling as sensations climbed, she was breathless as she spoke. "Two men at once."

"Ah, now we're getting somewhere. Any preferences for the other man? Big? Little?"

That devious little brush moved the damp strap of her thong aside and dipped into her wetness. "Huge cock, that's all I care about." She thrust against the brush, then groaned as it moved away, leaving her empty and aching.

"I'll have to see what I can do about that." Hunt painted her nipples with her cream, taking his time to ensure the job was thorough and she was nearly sobbing as he judged them to be complete.

"Do you know what my fantasy is?"

She blinked as the brush quit teasing and she looked over to see him choose a bottle from the table. "No," she swallowed hard. "What is it?"

"I want to fuck your breasts." He dribbled almond-scented oil into his hands and began massaging it into her breasts. "And I want you to watch me as I do it."

He slung his leg over her body and it was then she realized why the bench was so low. It was the perfect height for him to stand over her without straining his back or legs. He finished massaging the oil into her skin before he reached for the zipper on his pants. His oily hands wrapped around his cock as it sprang free. His eyes slid closed and his breathing deepened as he cupped his balls and moved his hands until his skin was slick with oil. He released his erection, guiding it to rest between her shiny breasts. Victoria licked her lips at the sight of his impressive erection so close and yet so far.

Pushing her breasts together, he created a slick tunnel. Rocking back and forth, he slowly began fucking her breasts as his thumbs teased her nipples and his eyes slid shut. A dreamy smile curved his mouth, as his motions grew languid, slow at times, then almost stilling. He was moving just enough to keep the sensation going but not enough to end it.

He was a beautiful man, she thought as she watched his face. Yes, he was physically beautiful, but she'd always known that. There was so much more to him, more than she'd ever dreamed. Her heart swelled as a warning buzzer sounded in her brain. Though she was treading in dangerous territory and her heart was at stake, she could have watched him for hours and hours.

All too soon his hips moved faster, his expression growing tense as the slap of his balls against her stomach increased. With a cry, he came, his cum splashing her chin and throat in warm spurts. His hips jerked several more times until he stilled. His eyes were still closed and his face and throat gleamed with sweat. Swaying slightly, his breathing was harsh as his body shook with aftershocks. Then, after a few moments, he opened his eyes and looked down at her.

"That was fantastic."

She forced a grin even as her vagina gave an unhappy twinge. "I'm glad you enjoyed it."

He tucked his cock into his pants before rubbing his cream into her breasts in slow, teasing strokes. "I'm glad you enjoyed it as well. However, I would imagine you're in need of further assistance."

She squirmed as he climbed off her. "You could put it that way."

He shrugged. "All you have to do is ask."

"Please, Master, get me off." It was all she could do to avoid begging. Her body ached with unfulfilled need and, while she needed a thick cock fucking her into oblivion, right now she'd take whatever he offered.

"How can I refuse when you ask so nicely?"

He moved between her thighs and, at the first brush of his tongue, she came with a wild screech. Her body, aroused for so long, was greedy and she took everything he gave. Again and again, he took her, his mouth against her flesh, his fingers buried deep within her. With each orgasm, her hips spanked the leather-padded bench with enthusiasm.

After several orgasms, each more powerful than the last, she collapsed, her body replete. "No more," she gasped. "No more, I can't take it."

She heard him chuckle. "As you wish my pet." Her body hummed with satisfaction and she couldn't bring herself to move as Hunt released her from her bonds. He scooped her up from the bench and carried her to a brocade couch where they stretched across the soft fabric.

With the scent of their lovemaking embedded in their skin, Victoria closed her eyes and enjoyed the feel of his arms around her. She'd found the perfect Master.

Now, if she could only bear to walk away in the morning.

Chapter Six

Hunt had never meant to fall in love with her. What had started out as a pleasant attraction had turned into more, so much more. Indulge in a delicious obsession, yes. Fall in love, no.

Oh, the attraction had been there from day one. Victoria was a beautiful, intelligent woman and any man would be a fool, including himself, to not snatch her up. There was no question in his mind that he wanted her to stay. But the decision was hers. Would she want to continue their relationship after tonight?

Hunt chose a white T-shirt and pulled it on, disturbed at the thought of her not being with him. Even in as short a period of time as what they'd had, he'd grown used to curling beside her. He enjoyed the way her perfume hung in the air after she'd left the room, the sound of her laughter and her beaming smile. Her sexy little blushes turned him on and the sounds she made when she came were enough to send him over the edge every time.

He also knew her well enough to know that, in her eyes, the reality of their situation was difficult. They did have a working relationship and there was a great deal of money, mostly his, involved. But he didn't care about that. As his lover, she'd be even more careful with his account than she was now. But, knowing her as he did, he also knew she'd see their relationship as a conflict of interest. But he'd talk to her about that later.

He slipped a belt around his waist and secured it. Now he had a guest who was soon to arrive and one woman's dream to make a reality.

* * * * *

A low fire crackled in the fireplace and Victoria was enjoying the warmth of the blaze along with a small glass of Grand Marnier. She'd chosen a pale pink shift to wear on their last evening together, knowing the soft color would enhance her pale coloring. Even though she'd only been wearing the scanty dresses a few days, already they seemed like a second skin to her. She didn't think she could ever go back to her figure-concealing clothing once she left Hunt's home in the morning.

Her heart gave an odd little pang at the thought of leaving. Did she really want to leave? Hunt had shown her so much, but there was more to be learned and he was the right man to teach her. But what did he want? So far he'd made no mention of continuing their relationship. Maybe, in his mind, this had only been meant as a weekend fling.

The doorbell sounded and she glanced outside to see a sleek black Lexus in the drive. Was Hunt expecting a visitor? He hadn't mentioned anything to her. She just hoped they didn't stay too long as this was her last night with him and she didn't want to waste it. She rose from her seat by the fire as she heard voices in the entry.

"Victoria, I'd like you to meet someone." Hunt entered with another man right behind him. "This is my brother, David." He came to her side and slid his arm around her waist, anchoring her against him. "David, this is Victoria."

Her jaw dropped. He was Hunt's exact double.

"You're a twin," she said.

David laughed. "Surely my brother told you?"

"No, he didn't." She looked from one to the other.

"Surprise." Hunt kissed her temple and she caught a whiff of his clean masculine scent. Her toes curled as he released her. "Come, brother, let's break bread. It's been a while since we've seen each other."

She fell into step just behind them as they walked to the dining room. Both men were mouth-wateringly gorgeous. Both were over six feet with the same dark brown hair and blue eyes. But their similarity ended there. David's hair was longer and he had the broad build of a weightlifter, while Hunt had the wiry build of a runner. And from this angle, she definitely had the best side of both men right in front of her. Their butts were high and taut, simply perfect.

The scent of roasted meat caused her stomach to growl loudly and she pressed her hand to her belly.

"What have you been doing, brother? Keeping this woman so busy you don't feed her?" David's eyes held a mischievous light as he slid his arm around her, his big hand landing on her hip. "Come, little one, let David assist you. Hunt won't tell you this, but I'm the good, kind brother." He pulled out a chair and ushered her into it.

"Is that so?" She grinned as he picked up the napkin and flicked it open, spreading it across her lap.

"Ah yes. My brother there, he got all the business acumen, but I received all the charm." David took the seat to her left while Hunt took the seat on her right. "Needless to say, he has all the money and I have all the fun."

Charmed, she laughed. "I'll bet you do, David."

"Don't let his good ol' boy act fool you, darling. David is an acclaimed artist when he isn't charming ladies out of their panties." Hunt picked up a bottle of wine and filled their glasses.

Victoria's skin heated at the reminder of her panty-less state. It would seem that both brothers had inherited that particular talent. She accepted the glass Hunt offered, enjoying the zing that ran down her arm as their fingers brushed.

As they ate dinner, conversation slowly turned to business and she was fascinated to hear that David knew almost as much about the shipping business as his brother. His comments revealed a sharp intelligence, which belied his earlier comment about his brother having all the brains. Both men were good looking, intelligent and excellent conversationalists.

She took a sip of her wine. There were definitely much worse ways to spend the evening.

After dinner David topped their wineglasses before they ventured back into the living room. Outside a soft rain was falling. With the fire burning, the wine in her system left Victoria feeling very comfortable. She curled on the couch next to Hunt, leaning into him as he laid his hand on her thigh. She set her glass down and leaned her head against his shoulder. He and David were talking about the latest football game, something she knew very little about.

Hunt stroked her thigh through the soft material of her dress, the movement soothing and sensual. Their voices faded to a pleasant buzz as she concentrated on the man beside her, his touch, his scent.

"I think we're putting your woman to sleep." Her eyes flew open to meet David's amused gaze. He grinned at his brother. "We're losing our touch. We used to get a woman into bed before we let her fall asleep."

Victoria grinned at his teasing. "Oh, you did, did you? Together? Now there's a thought. And how many women did you naughty boys manage to get into bed?"

"More than you'd think." Hunt's fingers slipped beneath her skirt, then slid upward, baring her thigh.

A jolt of awareness ran through her and her cunt clenched at the thought of these two handsome creatures taking her. She didn't miss David's interested gaze on her bared leg as Hunt moved her skirt higher.

She shifted her hips slightly, allowing him better access to her bare thigh. "And how did you get these women into your bed?"

Hunt's gaze clashed with hers and a rush of excitement pooled in her lower abdomen. "Charm, my dear." He slid his hand to the inside of her thigh.

She fought the urge to resist him and, for a split second, she tensed her thighs, not allowing him any higher than her inner knee. His glance turned inquiring and, in the depths of his gaze, she saw reassurance and something she wasn't sure she wanted to put a name to.

He dipped his head toward her. "This is *your* fantasy," he whispered.

Yes, it was and she wanted it, badly.

She relaxed her legs and his hand continued, teasing her to open for him. A wicked spiral of lust moved through her body as his hand brushed the top of her thigh. Her breasts tightened and her nipples ached and she wanted to rub herself against him like a cat. She glanced at David to find his heavy-lidded gaze glued to the path of his twin's hand. She wanted to be sandwiched naked between these two brutes and allow them to have their wicked way with her. She wanted all of it, and she wanted it now.

Her pulse took off as Hunt leaned close and kissed her. It was a soft kiss, measuring, tasting before changing, turning darker. His tongue slipped into her mouth, gliding over hers, teasing and tempting as their tongues began a sensual duel. She moaned when he pulled away from her.

"Well, little brother," Hunt said. "Maybe you'd like to sample some of this?"

Through narrowed eyes, Victoria watched David rise, the front of his jeans tented nicely. If he were as big as his brother...oh my, was she in for an experience.

Hunt pulled her into his lap as David approached. Her knees slid outside of Hunt's and he opened his legs, forcing hers open as well. David's dark gaze dropped to her exposed pubis and he licked his lips.

"She's hot for us, brother." He pulled off his shirt and tossed it to the side. Her eyes widened as she saw pierced nipples. How exotic!

"Yes, my Victoria is a firecracker." Hunt kissed her shoulder as David sank to his knees between her splayed thighs. "Be careful you don't get burned."

David's big hands landed on her waist as his mouth descended over hers, taking her softly at first, then with increasing heat. Behind her, Hunt was unbuttoning her dress, kissing every inch of skin he exposed as he worked his way down. Her top gapped and she raised her hands to prevent the material from sliding.

David broke the scorching kiss. "No, I want to see you." He removed her hands, allowing her bodice to slide, baring her breasts to his gaze. "Beautiful, very beautiful."

From behind, Hunt slid his hands around to cup her breasts, as if to offer them to his brother. She leaned back against his chest and felt wonderfully wanton as David's mouth latched onto an erect nipple. She moaned and squirmed against Hunt as his twin's talented mouth laved and suckled her erect flesh. She started to raise her hands to touch David only to realize that her arms were held captive by her dress and Hunt's arms. The feeling of restraint sent a rush of liquid heat through her cunt. Pinned between these two handsome creatures, she was a vessel to be filled only at their command. She ground her hips against Hunt's lap.

"Victoria," Hunt suckled her earlobe, wrenching a cry from her. "Do you want us to fuck you?"

His low, roughly worded question sent a gush of liquid heat directly to her core. Their hands moved over her body, touching her everywhere but where she really needed to be stroked. She tipped her head back and closed her eyes.

Warm lips nibbled at her throat.

Hunt.

While another pair of lips teased the inside of her knee. *David.* The men touched and stroked her until she was consumed with need. She knew instinctively that neither would touch her cunt until she told them what she wanted.

"Yes," she gasped. "I want you to fuck me, both of you." She opened her eyes in time to see David send Hunt a triumphant look, but she didn't care. All she wanted was a cock between her thighs. Something to drive away the ache that was slowly making her mad.

David stood and pulled her to her feet where she swayed dizzily. He pulled her into his arms and the press of his nipple rings against her chest was erotic as his mouth took hers. He was quite the kisser, almost as good as Hunt. Her arms still trapped, she leaned into him, giving as good as she got. Their tongues tangled as she felt Hunt press into her from behind. She moaned into David's mouth as she felt the heat of his brother's bare body against her back. She pushed against him as she felt the heat of his hard cock against her buttocks while David pressed his jeans-covered cock rhythmically into her mound.

She was turned around and Hunt took possession, her sensitized breasts rubbing his chest as their mouths mated. She leaned closer as his big hands moved, stroking every inch of exposed skin except where she really wanted him to touch her.

She heard the clang of a belt hitting the hearth just a second before a naked David snuggled from behind her, his big cock pressing into her. He rubbed against her, cradling his rod in the cleft of her buttocks. His hands cupped her breasts, squeezing then pinching her nipples.

Oh yes, this was what she wanted...

Hunt's hand moved between her thighs and she sobbed his name as he touched her erect clit. If she hadn't been pinned between them, she'd have melted into a boneless puddle of lust on the floor. His hand was joined by his twin's as he teased her damp opening. Her knees wobbled dangerously as David slid first one finger inside, then a second one followed.

"She's ready for us." His words were hot in her ear.

"Yes. Come, Victoria. Let us fuck you now," Hunt said.

He picked her up and carried her to a straight-backed wooden chair. It had a tall back and it was plain of any ornamentation save a notch cut into the front center of the seat. She'd noticed the chair before, thinking it somewhat out of place in the living room, but maybe it had been an antique. Hunt sat down and brought her with him, impaling her on his massive cock.

She let out a scream as he filled her. She tipped her head back, her breasts pressed into his chest. Hungry, their mouths ate at each other as his cock slowly moved in and out of her hungry cunt. Their tongues danced as their lower bodies mated. He grabbed her inner thighs and stretched her wide as he broke the kiss. His head dipped down to watch the slide of his cock into her cunt as he fucked her.

Behind her, she felt David press into her back. Something warm rushed down her spine and the scent of almond oil teased her senses. He rubbed the oil into her skin with strong deft movements and she turned to liquid butter in his capable hands. His fingers slipped into the crack of her ass to massage her rear entry.

She tensed immediately.

"She's not ready for that, brother," Hunt advised.

"Have you been plugging her?"

"Only with the smallest one."

David nodded and lightly bit her shoulder. "I'll just use a finger then."

Victoria knew she should be mortified. This talk of plugging someone was new and decidedly wicked, but she couldn't bring herself to object. This was her fantasy come true and then some.

Warm liquid slid down her crack and she pressed forward as David gently massaged it into her rear. The sensation was odd, though not unpleasant. She closed her eyes and willed her body to relax. As Hunt continued with slow thrusts, David entered her from the rear with one thick digit. That was all it took to push her over the edge. Her body tightened around both men as she screamed her pleasure, the rippling waves sending shudders through her body and she dimly thought they would never cease.

Limp, she felt both men pull away and she was aware that Hunt was still hard as a rock. Big hands turned her around until she sat on Hunt's lap facing David. Looking down, she then realized what the notch in the chair was for. One man could take a woman from behind while the other fucked her cunt. Ingenious...

Hunt's cock filled her from behind as David moved forward. He ran his fingers over her breasts before taking a nipple into his mouth. He suckled one, then the other as she squirmed beneath Hunt's slow, inexorably driving cock.

David released her mouth then pressed his cock against her mound. Mimicking his brother's movements, Victoria lost her breath as the twin pressures of the men threatened to send her over the edge. Four pairs of hands squeezed her breasts and stroked her back and stomach. Her entire body had turned into a ravenous sexual organ that knew no beginning or end. She existed simply to be filled and completed.

Behind her, she felt Hunt stiffen, his grip tightening on her waist as his hot seed spurted into her hungry vagina. It was enough to send her over the edge as well. As her shudders subsided, she rested against Hunt, her eyes half-closed. She stirred only when the men lifted her, removing Hunt's magnificent spent cock from her body. Hunt spread his legs and she felt the hard edge of the chair beneath her buttocks.

She forced open her eyes as David spread her thighs wide, bringing her knees up to her shoulders, pinning them there with his arms as his big hands held onto the edges of the broad seat. As he entered her, she arched her back, digging her shoulders into Hunt as David's hips set a mesmerizing pace.

Hunt's hands stroked and played with her nipples as he urged his brother on.

"Come on, David, fuck that cunt."

"I want to see her come for you."

"Yeah…just like that… she likes that…"

Victoria screamed her pleasure, once, then again as David continued his sensual assault on her body. She'd lost complete sense of self as they took her again and again, tossing her body over the edge of ecstasy.

David came hard, his hips hammering hers as he groaned. His movements slowed and he came to rest against her, his head on her shoulder. Victoria leaned her head back against Hunt and closed her eyes. Against her back she could feel his heartbeat and against her left breast, David's.

* * * * *

"Mmm." Victoria stirred when Hunt climbed into their bed after seeing his twin off. "I like your brother."

He chuckled. "I'll bet you do." He pulled down the sheets, baring her to his gaze. He ran his hand down her stomach, enjoying the way she moved beneath his touch. "Are you sore?"

"No." Her dark gaze met his through narrow eyes. "What did you have in mind?"

His hand came to rest on her mons. "Can you take me again?"

"Do you even have to ask?" She opened to him. "Come inside."

He entered her slowly, her flesh damp and slick. She smelled of sex and pool water. After their interlude in the living room, they'd all climbed in the heated pool to swim and play in the soft rain. Later they'd come upstairs and curled together in his bed. After David had drifted off to sleep, he and Victoria had snuck away for a quickie in the playroom before returning in time for David to wake up and take his leave.

"Mmm," she arched her hips. "After all our activity, I'm surprised you want me again."

"How could I not want you?" He didn't tell her it was the scorching kiss his brother had given her before he'd left. In the past, he and his brother had shared many women, but never one like Victoria. For the first time in his life, he'd been jealous of his brother as he watched him kiss Victoria good-bye. He didn't want her going to sleep with David's taste on her mouth or with David having given her the final orgasm of the night.

"Because you're tired? Because you've had me three times already?" She wrapped her legs around his waist. "That feels heavenly."

He settled into a slow thrust, his mouth teasing hers as they took their time climbing the slope. When they crested, their cries mingled and their bodies strained.

Hunt rolled to his side, careful to stay embedded in her flesh. In the morning, he'd talk to her about continuing their relationship, but for now he just wanted to enjoy the feel of her sleeping in his arms.

Tomorrow would come soon enough.

Chapter Seven

Victoria's shoulders sagged as she glanced at the Caller ID box attached to the phone. Recognizing the number of an old friend, she walked away, thankful when her voice mail picked up and the apartment fell silent.

She'd left Hunt's house over thirty-six hours ago and he'd made no attempt to contact her. No calls. No emails.

Nothing.

Life was back to normal. She'd returned to work, attended her meetings, dealt with the usual raft of issues that cropped up in the busy office. She'd had lunch in her office in order to catch up. She'd nailed a contract worth tens of thousands of dollars that she'd been working on for the past few weeks. She should have been ecstatic.

Never had normal looked so dull.

She picked up her glass of wine and strolled to the window. Below her, the verdant green of Central Park was hidden by nightfall. Lights glittered in the buildings bordering the park and the sky was clear, flecked with the few stars that could penetrate the light pollution of the city. At Hunt's home, the stars would be magnificent.

She shook her head.

Regardless of how the sky looked there, she was here where she belonged. She walked to the couch and plopped down, stretching her legs in front of her, heels on the coffee table.

Besides, Hunt had never said that he actually wanted a relationship with her. He'd wanted to master her and she'd wanted him…No, asked him to show her more of his world.

"Now, Victoria." His voice was a liquid caress and she felt the tip of his cock press against the entrance of her sex. "What do you want me to do?"

"Enter me," she whispered.

"Master," he prompted.

"Enter me, Master."

She shivered at the thought of his broad, warm hands on her body. Her breasts ached. All too quickly she'd become accustomed to frequent, satisfying sex and her body mourned its loss. Oh well, she still had her collection of vibrators.

It isn't the sex you miss. It's him.

Her gusty sigh sounded abnormally loud. Damn, she hated it when her subconscious talked back. She did miss him, and it wasn't just the sex. His astute mind and quick wit had attracted her long before she'd gotten her first taste of his delicious body. He'd mastered her within minutes of touching her and he'd shown her more care and attention than all of her haphazard relationships combined.

She was in love with him.

Victoria sank further into the leather cushions. Okay, so she was in love with him. Big deal. That and fifty cents wouldn't get her a cup of coffee. Hunt had made no mention of his feelings or lack thereof toward her. Of course, she hadn't asked either.

Too afraid of being rejected?

Possibly.

Probably.

Most definitely.

Brad's rejection had hurt; there was no doubt about that. They'd been in a relationship for almost two years when he'd walked away without even a backward glance. He'd said he loved her, but he'd walked away in the end. At least when she and Hunt parted, he hadn't been a hypocrite.

Of course, the question now was, what did she do?

She knew when she'd gotten into this that she'd have to see him again. He was a client and there was no getting around that reality. His account was sizable, though it was no longer imperative to OSD's future. But she still didn't want to lose it. Maybe he'd agree to her shifting the account to Molly's plate. She was a pleasant accommodating woman who was very popular with the male clients —

And very beautiful...

A spurt of jealousy lanced her heart.

No, Molly wouldn't do at all.

Mentally she ran through the list of her employees only to come up empty. They were all excellent at what they did or she'd never have hired them. But none of them were suitable for handling Hunt's account.

Quit lying to yourself. You don't want to give up the account at all. You'd miss your only opportunity to see him, smell him, touch him, even if it's only to shake his hand.

Damn the voice of reason. She tossed her wine back and slapped the glass down. A relationship between her and Hunt was impossible, period. Get over it and move on, Victoria.

She reached for the remote and turned on the television, hoping to drown the voices of her heart that dared contradict her mind.

"Hey, William."

Hunt tucked the small box into his pocket and tamped his irritation as he turned to greet Victoria's youngest brother.

"Jimmy, good to see you again." The young man bore an uncanny resemblance to his sister. They had the same brown hair and eyes, though Victoria's was more golden than her brother's. Even the shape of their faces was similar.

"Are you here for a meeting with Vic?" he asked.

"As a matter of fact, I am." *Not that she knows it...*

"I'll walk you up. I need to drop off some papers to Molly." The men fell into step as they headed for the elevators. "Have you met Molly yet?"

"No, I can't say that I have."

"She is *hot*. I mean, really hot. I've been wanting to ask her out for the longest time."

Hunt stifled a grin. He could remember being only twenty-five and the biggest challenge of his life was asking out the right girl. He patted his pocket, feeling the lump of the box against his thigh. Come to think of it, he could relate right now.

"So are you going to ask her out?"

"Yep. Her favorite band is coming to town and I have tickets. How can she resist?"

Indeed.

The doors opened with a soft whoosh and they stepped out onto the administrative level. Jimmy led him toward Victoria's office. Her assistant looked up with a bright smile on her face that was quickly replaced with a look of confusion. She reached for her date book.

"Hey, Kelley. Mr. Hunter has an appointment with Victoria and I'll just walk him in," Jimmy said cheerfully.

"But... wait..." Kelley spluttered.

Jimmy ignored her, opened Victoria's door and just walked in. "Molly, fancy seeing you here."

"Jimmy, what do you —"

Her voice trailed off as Hunt entered. He inhaled the scent of her perfume as his gaze drank him in. She sat at her desk, her hair confined in a neat twist and her suit jacket carelessly tossed over the back of her chair. Her startled expression quickly smoothed into a cool, professional façade. Next to her sat a perky blonde with a pair of glasses perched on her nose.

"Mr. Hunter, what an unexpected surprise." She rose from her seat and started toward him.

"Ms. Brittain." Hunt took her hand and thwarted her attempt to shake by kissing her knuckles. The scent of lavender hand cream sent a shiver of arousal through his system. "You look beautiful this morning."

A soft flush colored her cheeks and she pulled her hand away. "Molly, if you could please excuse us. I need to meet with Mr. Hunter for a few minutes."

"Sure, Ms. Brittain." The perky blonde popped to her feet and gathered her planner and cup of coffee. "I'll be at my desk. Just call when you're ready to continue."

Hunt didn't miss her speculative glance as she left with an adoring Jimmy hot on her heels. He'd bet next week's receipts that no one in their office had ever seen the dragon-lady blush before.

"What can I do for you, Mr. Hunter?" Victoria sat at her desk and began pushing papers around. If he didn't know better, he'd think she was nervous.

"So tell me, Victoria. Are you wearing panties?" He sat on the edge of her desk, deliberately crowding her.

She leaned back in her chair, whether to put some space between them or to enable her to meet his gaze, he wasn't sure. "I don't see how that's any of your business now."

"You and I have unfinished business. No, we *are* unfinished business." He crossed his arms over his chest. "You left before we could discuss our future."

"We have a business relationship—"

"Bullshit."

She ignored him. "And we have to carry forward with it. If you wish, I can have your account transferred—"

"How can you sit there as if nothing happened between us?" He grabbed her arm and hauled her out of her chair. Startled, she was thrown off balance and had to lean into him to remain upright. Her palm scorched his chest. "I had my face in your pussy, you had my cock in your mouth and you came apart in my arms so many times that I lost count. Don't sit there and tell me you feel nothing for me."

"I never said that," she snapped.

"Well, then, what's the problem?"

"I-I-I-"

He saw the yearning in her eyes. "And don't lie to me."

"I want you," she whispered.

Dominique Adair

A rush of primal satisfaction ran through him. He knew she wanted him; she just had to admit out loud. She would never be able to accept a relationship with him unless she came to him of her own free will. Of course he was going to do everything in his power to give her a guiding hand.

"You have me." He reached for the pins in her hair and began pulling them out, allowing the silky mass to tumble about her shoulders. "Now what?"

"We have a working relationship—"

"You're fired." He nipped her throat and inhaled the scent of warm woman, his woman.

"You can't just fire me..." she spluttered.

"Fine, you're rehired." He unbuttoned the top buttons of her shirt and nuzzled her lace-covered breasts. "If you try to use our professional relationship as an excuse to keep from being involved with me, I'll fire you again."

"Ahhh."

She gasped as he plucked at her nipple. His gaze zeroed in on her face as her eyes went smoky with desire. He removed her shirt and bra, then tossed both on the floor. "I have a gift for you."

She blinked and raised her head. "You do?"

He removed the box from his pocket and opened it to reveal a gold chain with a loop on each end. He handed her the box, then teased her nipples with his fingers until they were rosy and erect. Taking one loop, he slid it over her nipple, tightening until it was secure. Repeating the procedure, he attached the other end until the gold chain hung suspended from her nipples.

"You have the most beautiful breasts I've ever seen. And now that you're wearing my gold, I'm telling the world that you're mine."

Victoria laughed and the chain jiggled. "Most women receive a ring."

"You'd wear a clit ring for me? Honey." He gave her a noisy kiss. "I didn't know you cared that much."

"Ugh, no piercings unless you're going to get a matching cock ornament." She tangled her fingers in his hair.

Inwardly he cringed. "Okay, scratch that idea." He grabbed her waist and swung her around until she was seated on the desk. Pressing her thighs apart, he snuggled his arousal against her mound. "Shall we christen your desk?"

"We've already done that."

"Mmm, but you weren't actually on the desk that time." He slid his hands up her thighs, skimming her firm flesh. "The panties have to go."

Her eyes gleamed with amusement and lust as she shimmied her hips and he slid them off. "While I do have an appreciation for ivory silk, I don't think they'll be needed now." He wadded them and shoved them into his pocket.

"And we won't be needing this anymore." Her nimble fingers attacked his buttons.

"If you insist." He chuckled, his breath caught in mid-gasp she tweaked his nipple. He unbuttoned his pants and allowed his cock to spring free. "Are you ready for this?" He rocked his hips, pressing his rigid member against the notch of her thighs.

"More than ever."

His breath caught as her slim fingers encircled him. In her gentle grasp, she guided his head to her dewy entrance. They stood close, their bodies bathed in combined heat as he entered her. His breathing became labored and he fought for control as her tight passage closed around him, drawing him in. He remained still, fighting for control.

"Hunt," she whispered. "I need you now."

He pushed in a fraction more, the feel of her tight cunt threatened to steal his breath away. Flexing his hips, he began moving within her. Slowly at first, then, at her exuberant urging, with a deeper thrust. Dimly he was aware of items hitting the floor from the top of her desk, but he couldn't care less. As long as no one tried to take this luscious woman from his arms and from around his cock, he didn't care if the building was in danger of coming down.

Capturing a nipple between his teeth, he leisurely sucked her tight flesh, eliciting a shriek from Victoria. As long as she wore her chain, her nipples would be overly sensitive to even the slightest touch. He groaned as her nails scored his skin as she came, sending him over the edge after her.

Later they collapsed in a tangled heap on the couch, their breathing ragged.

"Are you ready to leave work for the day?" He nuzzled her temple. "I think I'd like to take you home and dress you in a latex outfit I bought with you in mind."

"Latex?" she grinned. "Why not leather?"

"Latex and a bottle of oil can be a lot of fun."

"Sounds enticing." Victoria gave a throaty laugh as she dragged her nails across his chest. "Of course, I have a much more important question that we need to address. When do I get to tie you up?"

A rush of lust ran through Hunt and his cock gave a mighty twitch. He glanced at his Rolex. "How fast can we get out of here?"

ANNE'S BIRTHDAY BACHELOR

Written by

JENNIFER DUNNE

Chapter One

"I really envy her." Anne Logan pointed her salad fork at the spandex-sheathed bimbette two tables away.

Her best friend, Sarah, checked discreetly in her compact mirror to see who Anne was talking about. "Why? Because she's gorgeous, young, and has a wealthy man showering her with expensive gifts?"

"No. Because she's completely taken care of."

"And that's a good thing?"

"Just think about it. I mean, what does she have to do? Look beautiful, laugh at his jokes, and tell him he's an animal in bed. Hardly rocket science. And in return, he tells her what to wear, where to go, what to do…every decision made for her."

Sarah stared at her until Anne started to feel uncomfortable. "You mean it."

"I guess I do." Anne stabbed savagely at her salad, skewering hapless lettuce leaves. "Don't get me wrong. I love my business. I've built it from nothing to be one of the hottest advertising firms in the city. We were even short-listed for a Clio last year. But the downside of that is that it's my business. All of it. Every last little detail. I have to be consulted on campaign ideas, presentations, promotions, images, slogans, right down to thematic colors and type-fonts.

I have to make a decision on each and every one. And it has to be the right decision. I swear, if I didn't allow myself the indulgence of lunching with you once a month instead of always meeting with clients, I'd have gone insane long before now."

"You need to get laid."

Anne snorted. "Yeah, right. Like that would help. I've read all the books. I'm in control of my own orgasm. I need to tell my lover what pleases me, and how he can make me climax. Pfeh! More decisions. It's not worth it."

Sarah chewed on her lip, her chicken Caesar salad forgotten in the face of Anne's problem.

"Oh, forget about my whining. It's probably just PMS making me cranky. Eat already."

Slowly, Sarah resumed nibbling at her lunch. "You know, it's your birthday next Friday."

"Don't remind me. Now I'm not just overworked, I'm old and overworked."

"I'm serious. We should do something to celebrate. Why don't I take you out for dinner? Someplace new and exciting." Sarah wiggled her eyebrows lasciviously. "There's a new male strip club, supposed to be hot stuff."

Anne laughed. "I was looking forward to a quiet night with no overtime work from the office, but okay. Go ahead and twist my arm."

Back in the office, after lunch, Anne thought about what she'd told Sarah. Did she really want a man to take care of her? Not if it meant giving up control of her business. But it was a nice fantasy, to be completely and totally pampered and indulged, with no obligations other than pleasing her man.

She smiled and lightly stroked the eraser of the pencil she was holding over her lips. Would his lips brush hers, softly, like so? She licked her bottom lip, and the eraser slicked the moisture back and forth.

Her nipples tingled and tightened, as if her imagined lover was really kissing her. She thought about him reaching down to tease her nipples, tweaking them lightly with his strong fingers, then claiming them with his teeth and tongue.

Anne's breath sped up, and her sex grew heated. She was wearing a chic, stylish miniskirt, and she imagined her fantasy lover telling her to sit on the edge of her desk with her legs spread so that it rode up to her hips. He would reach between her legs, stroking the soft skin of her inner thigh with teasing circles.

Moisture dampened her panties. She imagined her faceless, nameless lover zipping open his pants and releasing himself. Her throat dried up as she visualized his long, thick penis, a bead of pearly cum already gleaming at its tip.

Would he tell her to kiss it? Lick it? Suck it? Or would he just slam it into her, demanding her body's surrender as his right?

In her mind, he grabbed her hips, holding her where he wanted her, and thrust into her with a force that rocked her backward and pulled a cry from her lips.

"Say you want me," he growled.

"I want you."

He thrust into her a second time.

"Say you need me."

"I need you."

A third time he pulled back and slammed his cock home, sheathing himself so deeply that his coarse pubic hair tickled her sensitive clitoris.

"Say you'll do anything for me."

"I'll do anything for you. Just tell me what you want me to do."

He started sliding in and out of her, pushing her back and forth on the desk in time with his movements, and angling his strokes so that she felt the heavy, wet head of his cock forcing its way up the walls of her vagina.

"Then do this for me. Don't move. And don't come."

Anne stiffened, holding herself rigid instead of rocking with his thrusts. The only part of her that moved was the flesh beneath his onslaught, and she felt every stretch of tight skin like a burning fire that threatened to consume her.

Her lover grunted and continued thrusting into her, inhumanly hot and hard. He pushed her backwards, sprawling her onto her desk and knocking a flurry of pens and papers to the floor. Bending over her, he followed her down. As he thrust into her, even deeper than before, he bit her swollen nipple.

Anne gasped as lightning connected her breast to his thrusting cock. She tried to remain motionless, but her hips and legs started to tremble.

He slid almost all the way out, then rammed his cock home and bit her other nipple.

"I can't do it," she moaned. "I can't stay still."

"Just...a...little...longer," he grunted between thrusts.

She moaned with pleasure, tears leaking from the corners of her eyes as she struggled to obey.

He grabbed her legs and pulled them tight against his hips. "Lock your legs around my waist."

Fully sheathed within her, he pulled her up, off the desk, so she was riding him, gravity impaling her on his huge cock, and pressed her up against the wall. His hips swiveled, rolling his cock inside her, faster and faster. The tears streamed down her face as she gasped and panted.

Since he'd pinned her against the wall, he didn't need his hands to hold her, and he slid his hands up under her miniskirt, cupping and caressing her ass. He pressed the fingers of one hand into her opening, reaching inside her so that she could feel his fingers and his cock trapping her throbbing flesh between them. He was loving her from both sides, and she thought she'd die from the pleasure.

Then he kissed her. Hard, punishing kisses bruised her lips until he bit the swollen skin and drew hot blood. And still his fingers and his cock possessed her. He forced open her mouth allowing his tongue to slip inside. Pulling her tongue into his mouth, he sucked her in time with his thrusts.

"Now," he said, releasing her tongue long enough to speak. "Now you may come."

He threw his head back, the cords of his neck standing in sharp relief, as his body tensed for his final thrust. He spilled his seed in a geyser of heat, triggering her own rush of fluid in wave after shuddering wave.

Anne blinked, returning to awareness, to find she was still seated behind her desk at work, fully clothed with the door of her office wide open. Her panties were soaked, and she'd snapped the pencil she'd been holding, but there were no other signs of the heated encounter she'd just imagined. Most importantly, she apparently hadn't said anything out loud, because no crowd of employees gathered around her door to see what all the shouting and moaning was about.

She dropped the broken pencil and ran a shaky hand through her hair. "The problem with being an artist," she muttered, "is an overdeveloped visual imagination."

More importantly, her flight of fancy proved that Sarah had been right. Anne really did need to get laid, before her distraction started affecting her work.

She thought of the men she knew and couldn't work up enough interest to call any of them. Sex with them was never as good as her imagined sex with her mystery lover. She may as well save herself the grief and frustration, and just schedule a half hour of good vibrations from her micro-massager.

Smiling, Anne blocked off a half-hour massage on her calendar for that evening.

* * * * *

Sarah called her up a couple of times over the next few days to discuss possible outings for her birthday celebration, but seemed to forget about it once the weekend rolled around. Anne was glad. She'd dreaded planning the proposed celebration. Where did she want to eat? What show did she want to see? What time did she want to go out? How much did she want to spend? Too many decisions, all pointless and picayune, yet all needing to be made. It was her birthday, and she should be able to spend it however made her happiest.

She'd like to just stay home, order takeout from the deli—she always ordered the grilled chicken salad, mustard vinaigrette on the side, so that didn't require a decision—and watch whatever movie was being broadcast on network TV. When Sarah still hadn't called her by lunchtime the next Friday, Anne started looking forward to her quiet, decision-less evening.

The phone rang just after three o'clock.

"Hey, Anne! Happy birthday!"

"Sarah! I didn't expect to hear from you."

"Tonight's your birthday celebration. You didn't think I'd forget about that, did you?"

"Well, when you stopped calling to plan, I'd hoped…"

Sarah laughed. "It's because I didn't need to plan any more. I came up with the perfect celebration."

"What?" Cold dread spiraled down Anne's back. Just because she wanted a break from constant decision-making didn't mean she wanted to be a doormat. Since Sarah's previous brilliant ideas had included full-body henna tattoos and the humiliating spa treatment that included French Country Showers, a fancy name for standing naked and covered in mud in the center of a room while spa employees hosed you down, Anne instinctively distrusted any celebration Sarah thought was perfect.

"I went to that charity bachelor auction last weekend, to raise money for the burn unit at the hospital."

"Tell me you didn't do what I think you did."

"I did. I bought you a bachelor."

"Sarah!" Anne stood up and closed her office door. No way did she want her employees hearing what she had to say to her friend. "I told you I didn't want to get laid."

That wasn't true, of course. She'd dreamt of her imaginary lover several times in the intervening week, how he commanded her body and soul until he brought her to a tearful, screaming climax, again and again. But he was just a fantasy. No real man could possibly compare with her imagination. While she longed for his commanding arrogance in the bedroom, that personality would make him an insufferable jerk the rest of the time.

"Relax, Anne," Sarah said. "The rules of the auction are very clear. He's supposed to take the winner out to dinner, and that's all that's being auctioned."

Anne groaned. "Great. So instead of a nice quiet birthday celebration, I get to make awkward small-talk with a guy who was roped into the date for charity. And I don't even get any sex for my trouble. Why did you think I would find this at all appealing?"

"The bachelors had to give little speeches about what kind of date they would take the winner on. Garrett described a date where he pampered the winner and took care of her every need, and I immediately thought of your comments at lunch."

"He probably meant he'd bring me flowers, open the door for me, and pull out my chair. That wasn't what I was looking for, and you know it."

"I don't think so." Sarah's voice took on a lilting quality, as if she knew a secret she wasn't going to share.

"C'mon, Sarah. Give. What's up with the date, really?"

"I'm not saying. But he's coming to pick you up for dinner at six. Wear something sexy."

* * * * *

Anne checked her hair one last time, then resumed pacing her living room. She never should have let Sarah talk her into this. Going out on a blind date with a charity bachelor was a stupid idea. Getting breathless with anticipation, wondering if he'd be anything like her imaginary lover, was practically guaranteeing disappointment.

Still, she'd followed Sarah's suggestion, determined to play along with the fantasy of being a bimbette for the night. She wore a micro-miniskirt of butter soft black leather, and a clinging angora sweater with a neckline that plunged almost to her navel. If she turned the right way, you could just catch glimpses of the black lace bra she was wearing underneath it.

Her skin was spritzed with rose musk oil, and shimmering powder highlighted her throat and breasts. Her black pantyhose had tiny roses stitched into the weave, accenting her long legs, which were made longer by the high-heeled black strappy shoes.

The doorbell rang before she had a chance to obsess about her appearance any further. Taking a deep, calming breath, she opened the door.

Garrett was 6'2" with short dark hair, his dark-and-dangerous look enhanced by black slacks, black collarless shirt, and charcoal sport jacket. But what captivated Anne's attention was the barely leashed energy that blazed from his dark eyes. This man could set the city on fire if he chose. And tonight, he was choosing to focus that intensity on her.

Recalling her manners, she stepped aside from the door. "Come on in. I'm Anne."

"Thank you. I'm Garrett." His voice was low and husky, just made for whispering sweet nothings in the wee hours of the morning. Closing the door behind himself, he said, "Sarah gave me a lot of information for this date, and I want to make sure you and she were in synch before we went any further."

"Oh?" That was a nice, noncommittal answer. Honestly, how did he expect her to discuss anything with him when all she could think about was running her fingers through that thick hair?

"She said you were looking for someone to take control, to make all the decisions and tell you what to do."

Anne blinked. "Yeah, that's what I said. But I didn't expect anyone would actually want to do that. Not for just a dinner date."

Garrett grinned, the expression transforming him from merely good looking to devilishly handsome. His teeth were brilliant white, and she could just imagine them nipping and biting her the way she dreamed. And his dark brows, slanting over glinting eyes, suggested that he knew exactly what she'd fantasized about.

"That's a game I like to play, whenever I get the chance. Whether it's just for a dinner or for a whole night long doesn't change its appeal."

Anne swallowed the lump that had formed in her dry throat. "Oh."

"If you'd like to play, too, here are the rules. Beginning when we walk out that door, until we return from dinner, you let me control where we go, what we do, and how we do it. And I mean, I won't ask for your opinion on anything, although if there's something you really object to you can stop playing anytime, just by saying 'Game Over.' But while the game's on, all you need to do is look gorgeous." His gaze swept her clinging sweater and tight skirt. "That'll be easy enough for you."

She felt her pulse speeding up, and her skin growing warm with expectation. "Sarah said there were very strict rules about the dates."

Garrett nodded. "Just dinner. Not even a kiss, except a goodnight kiss at the end of the date is allowed."

Oh, well. It was too much to expect that he'd be able to fulfill her sexual fantasy. This was still going to be more than she'd ever expected having in real life.

Anne held out her hand, hoping Garrett couldn't see her trembling with anticipation. "I'll play. As soon as we walk out that door, you'll become my lord and master, and I will be completely subservient to your will."

"It's a deal, then." His warm hand closed around hers, sealing the agreement. "Happy birthday, Anne."

Chapter Two

Garrett settled Anne into his car, a high-end black BMW with a leather interior. The back of his hand brushed her breasts as he pulled out her seat belt and fastened it for her. The corner of his mouth quirked upward, letting her know that the "accidental" touch had been no accident, and his bold gaze promised that he'd find plenty of excuses for touching her, regardless of the charity's strict terms about their date.

Anne's nipples tightened with anticipation. When would he touch her again? And how?

Garrett's gaze dipped down to the tight buds clearly outlined beneath her clinging sweater, and his smile broadened. "We're going to have fun tonight," he promised.

The fun began on their drive to the restaurant. Taking full advantage of the BMW's manual transmission, Garrett shifted often in the city's stop and go traffic, his fingers or the back of his hand fluttering against the outside of Anne's thigh with each gearshift. Pretending to notice nothing, Anne casually spread her legs, nudging her thigh closer to his hand.

The erratic and fleeting caresses teased her more than she would have imagined, and she found herself anticipating red lights with eager hunger, hoping for another quick downshift. At one light, Garrett grabbed her knee "by mistake," then trailed a stroke of lightning with his fingernails up the inside of her thigh in his blind quest for the BMW's stick.

Anne let out her breath in a shaky sigh. Oh, he was good at this game. Very good.

They pulled into the parking lot of Paloma's, a trendy restaurant that mixed country French cooking with high fashion and art. Garrett's BMW looked perfectly at home in the lot full of Mercedes, Porsches, and BMWs, with a few Lincolns, Buicks and Range Rovers dotting the mix.

She waited breathlessly for him to circle the car and release her, hoping he'd stroke her breasts again. He leaned over and unsnapped her seatbelt, and she arched forward, presenting an appealing target. Instead, he pulled the belt wide before releasing it, neither his hands nor the fabric strap coming anywhere near her chest.

"Remember," he cautioned. "I'm in control here."

Anne nodded, accepting his chastisement. No overt suggestions from her would be allowed. But subtle encouragement, like moving her leg closer to his hand, was okay. "Whatever you say."

Garrett took her hand to help her from the car, rubbing his thumb over her knuckles, then circling one of the joints while gazing heatedly at her breasts. She could imagine his thumb was circling her nipple, soft and slow, then flicking across with sharp strokes.

Her breath hitched, and she felt her nipples tightening again, tingling as if he was truly teasing the hot tips of her breasts instead of the knuckles on her hand.

He chuckled softly. "That's my girl. Now let's go inside and show you off to the world."

Her legs were weak enough that Anne actually needed the assistance of Garrett's strong hand pulling her to her feet. Then he led her toward the restaurant's front door, his hand resting in the small of her back.

She hesitated by a strip of torn up pavement temporarily filled with loose gravel. Garrett instantly stopped beside her.

"Is there a problem?"

"My shoes..." Anne considered her thin, strappy heels, and the looming pit of gravel. She could probably get through without twisting her ankle, but she was certain to get at least one pebble between the sole of her foot and the thin Italian leather.

Garrett stepped behind her, his hands spanning her waist and one muscular leg braced between hers, then lifted her up and over the construction.

Anne blinked, surprised at the sudden transition, and blurted out the first thing that came into her head. "My, you're strong."

"I work out regularly at the gym." He stepped across the gravel and rejoined her, caressing her hip briefly before returning his hand to its previous position on her back. "I could bench press your pretty little body for hours without breaking a sweat."

An image sprang to her mind, of him on his back on a weight lifting bench, naked, raising and lowering her over his erection. Effortlessly. She swallowed, and rubbed her hands together to disperse the sweaty feeling in her palms. Her masterful imaginary lover now wore Garrett's face.

He steered her across the rest of the lot and up the stairs with subtle pressure from his fingertips and the heel of his palm, as if he was leading her in a dance. Anne realized with surprise, that was exactly what he was doing. They were partners in the age old dance of male and female, and he was leading her through the steps. Tonight, the dance would end with the dancers bowing and going their separate ways, according to the charity auction's rules, but if they enjoyed the evening, there was no reason they couldn't have another date, with a different ending.

Garrett held the door for her, ushering her through. She waited for him in the vestibule, her back suddenly cold without the reassuring weight of his hand. When he rejoined her, his hand once again settling against her back, she smiled up at him.

"What's that for?" he asked.

"I'm just happy."

He pulled her ever so slightly toward him in a loose, one-handed hug. "The night is young."

They walked through the blue and yellow vestibule, admiring the framed watercolors of daffodils and lilies, until they reached the hostess station. Garrett pulled his hand away from Anne's back, and she obediently stopped, waiting for further directions.

"Chantrell, reservation for two," Garrett told the woman standing behind the station. She crossed his name off of her list, and picked up two leather-clad menus.

"If you'll follow me, please?"

Anne waited until a gentle pressure from Garrett's hand urged her forward. As he guided her through the tangle of tables after the hostess, Anne wondered how the other diners saw them. They probably thought Garrett's hand on her back was a chivalrous gesture of protection, never realizing that it was a master's touch directing his slave.

Her blood heated as she realized they played their game in full view of the surrounding diners, yet none of them knew what was going on. That's why Garrett didn't want her to make any overt suggestions. Their game was all the spicier because it was a secret, hidden in plain sight.

They took their seats at a secluded table in the garden room, surrounded by *trompe l'oil* ivy and roses so realistic they seemed the source of the vase of pink and peach roses in the center of each table. Anne accepted her menu from the hostess, waiting until

Garrett had his before opening it. A light tap of his shoe against her ankle got her attention.

She looked up in surprise. "What?"

"Put your menu down. No decisions, remember?"

Obediently, she closed her menu and set it on the table. It was what she'd asked for. But their game didn't seem like quite so much fun now, not when her health and well-being might be on the line. She consoled herself with the knowledge that if he chose something she couldn't eat, she could always stop playing.

Confident that she could stop him before he placed an order for anything she was allergic to, Anne relaxed into her role. While he studied his menu, she studied him.

He had strong hands, with long, lean fingers — pianist's hands, she'd heard them called. A heated flush swept over her skin as she imagined him playing her body, evoking a symphony of passion.

She grabbed her water glass and drained it in three long swallows. When she set the glass back on the table, it contained only chunks of ice and a lonely looking sliver of lemon.

Their waiter appeared a moment later to give them the list of daily specials and take their order. She avoided making eye contact, hoping he'd realize Garrett would place the orders for both of them.

Instead, he turned to her. "Madame?"

"The lady will have the steak in burgundy mushroom sauce, medium well," Garrett answered. "And instead of the noodles, an extra side of vegetables."

"Very good, monsieur. And for you?"

"I'll have the poached grouper."

"An excellent choice." The waiter gathered the menus. "Your salad course will be out shortly."

A different waiter came by and refilled her water glass, then a third brought them a basket of rolls and decoratively shaped breadsticks. Garrett halted him with a hand gesture.

"My companion is unable to eat wheat flour. Do you have any breads that are gluten-free?"

Anne's eyes widened in surprise, then she gave herself a mental kick. Of course Sarah would have told Garrett about her food allergies. That's probably also how he knew she loved anything in a burgundy sauce.

Still, as she helped herself to one of the slices of unleavened flat bread that the waiter had returned with, the last of her reservations about abandoning herself to Garrett's control faded away. She had complete confidence in his ability to care for her. And if only the charity hadn't put that silly stipulation on their bachelors, she was confident he'd have proved equally able to satisfy her sexual fantasies.

"So what do you do when you're not being an eligible bachelor?" she asked.

"I'm a currency trader."

"Is that like banking?" He didn't seem at all the gray suit and green eyeshade type.

Garrett chuckled. "Hardly. It's more like the stock market, only with money."

"Do you like it?"

"I love it. It's like standing in the eye of a hurricane, never knowing when you might get swept away. An amazing rush. And I'm good at it. I'm on track to make partner in my firm in a few years."

Anne smiled, easily able to picture him wrestling the world currency markets into submission, like some financial Crocodile Hunter. "What happens when you make partner?"

"Same job, but a bigger cut of the profits. I'll also direct the traders under me, telling them what to look for and what our overall strategy will be. And, of course, I'll spend more time in one office. So far, I've worked in Tokyo, San Francisco and New York. I'll move on to London next, followed by a brief stop in Germany, then it's Partner City."

A sudden chill wiped away her smile. "When are you moving to London?"

"A couple of months." Garrett seemed to pick up on her tension, because he leaned forward, his expression serious. "We could have a lot of fun together in two months, but that's all it would be. Fun. Don't get your hopes up for anything long term."

Anne shook her head, and smiled brilliantly. "Of course not. I don't have time for any serious commitments, anyway. I've got to devote all my energies to my business. A little light fun to relax is just what I'm looking for."

Leaning back with a pleased smile, he asked, "So tell me about this business of yours. Sarah said you ran an advertising agency."

"Yes." Now it was Anne's turn to lean forward in eagerness. She loved talking about her work, and her plans for the future. Her five year plan was ambitious, but she had faith in her ability to carry it out. Look how far she'd already come. Billion dollar accounts were well within the realm of possibility.

Their conversation drifted through various other topics, from current events to their individual memories of their high school years. Through it all, Garrett subtly reminded her of their game, stretching his legs to brush hers with a brief caress, or making gentle demands that she really must try this or that delicacy from his plate. Each reminder only served to whet her appetite for the moment when she would be completely under his control, with no curious diners surrounding them to block his inhibitions. What would he demand then?

The anticipation kept her in a euphoric state of near arousal. She paradoxically couldn't wait until she got him alone, and never wanted the delightful feelings to end. All too soon, their empty dishes were removed, and the waiter was scraping crumbs from the crisp linen tablecloth.

"Will you be having dessert? Coffee? Although we are known for our pastries, the chef has also created a fresh raspberry sorbet, or you can have fresh strawberries over a scoop of vanilla ice cream."

"No, thank you. Just the check."

"At once, monsieur."

As the waiter hustled off to get their check, Garrett swept his heated gaze over Anne. "I'd prefer to savor dessert somewhere more private."

She barely noted the waiter's return with the bill, then his second return with the charge slip. All she could think about was the promise in Garrett's words. What would he want to taste for dessert?

Soon, she was seated in his car again. His "accidental" stroke of her heated nipples with the cool metal of the seat belt nearly sent her over the edge. She wanted to grab him and kiss him as senseless as he made her, but that wasn't part of the game. Her role called for her to pretend nothing had happened — that her breasts were not hot and swollen, heavy and aching for his touch, that her panties were not damp with wanting his ultimate possession. The strain of not reacting only strengthened the intensity of her inner reaction, and the blood began to pulse between her legs, her body throbbing with eager anticipation of his next touch.

As if he knew how close she hovered to the edge, Garrett teased her with downshifting only twice during the drive back to her brownstone. Or maybe he was shooting through the amber lights in his hurry to return.

He pulled the BMW into one of the parking spots on the street in front of her home, then cut the engine and turned to face her.

"We're here. The date and the game, are officially over."

Anne blinked. This wasn't what she'd expected him to say. Her stunned mind fell back on well-rehearsed social niceties. "I had a wonderful time."

"So did I." Garrett reached over and freed her seat belt. The harness automatically retracted, sweeping the strap over her sensitive breasts.

She gasped.

He raised his hand, his palm hovering over her sweater so that she could feel the heat through the angora. She longed to arch her back and press her breast into his cupped hand. But she remained still, waiting for his direction.

He smiled, as if her non-reaction pleased him. "May I?"

Right. Their date was over. She was no longer bound to his will. The realization saddened her. "Please. Whatever you want."

He circled his palm over her breast, teasing the nipple to a hard peak. Then he reached inside the vee of her sweater, and stroked his fingertips over the lace of her bra.

Anne closed her eyes, drowning in the sensation. Garrett toyed with the lace a moment longer, then slipped his hand beneath the thin fabric to cup her breast. He lifted and released her breast from its containment, the tight elastic pressing the underside of her breast and raising it to his teasing touch. He cupped and fondled her, then rolled her nipple between his fingers. When he squeezed gently, sheets of flame engulfed her and she thought she'd come right there, sitting in his car.

His thumb flicked back and forth across her nipple, each sharp stroke wrenching a gasp from her laboring lungs.

"Like I said, the official bachelor auction date is over. But if you wanted to have a second date, starting now, it wouldn't have to follow any of their rules."

His meaning gradually became clear to her passion-fogged brain. A wave of eagerness swept through her, and she started to tremble with anticipation.

"Yes, please. I would like that very much." Then, in case there was any doubt, she added, "Come inside and make love to me."

Garrett chuckled, low in his throat. "I'd hoped you would say that. Just in case, I packed a bag with a few things you might find…entertaining."

Anne licked her dry lips. "Like what?"

"A few toys to reward my most willing servant for her excellent service."

He pinched her nipple, temporarily blinding her with a white-hot flash of desire. Anne blinked watering eyes, suddenly reminded of the way her mystery lover had brought her to one sobbing release after the other. Maybe Garrett would be able to fulfill all of her sexual fantasies after all.

"I'm yours to command."

Chapter Three

Garrett grabbed a black leather duffle bag from the BMW's trunk, then followed Anne up the stone steps into her home. Intriguing clinks and muffled rustlings came from within the bag as it swung beside him. Ignoring the expensive artwork dotting the foyer, placed there to impress and intimidate her clients during the holiday parties she hosted, she led Garrett directly to her bedroom.

He glanced around the room, considering. She wondered what the spare, modern lines of the Danish dresser, nightstand and matching headboard suggested to him. Normally, she loved the simplicity and order of the furniture. But now she regretted not going with the more traditional canopied four-poster.

After dropping his bag to the gleaming hardwood floor with a rattling clank, Garrett sat on her bed, sinking into the thick down comforter. "Sit. We need to talk."

Confused, Anne sat next to him. She'd expected him to take charge, demanding her surrender, and teasing her with whatever he'd brought in his bag until she shattered in blissful release. They'd spent all night talking. Now was the time for action.

Suddenly, she realized what his hesitation was for. "Don't worry. I have condoms."

He smiled, and stroked her cheek. "Sweet Anne. How considerate of you. But that's not what I wanted to talk to you about."

"It's not?"

"No. I always carry plenty. We need to talk about you, what you expect, desire, and fear. Is this the first time you've done this?"

"I've had sex before. But never as part of a game like we played at dinner."

He nodded. "I thought not. It can get pretty intense, and you might not be thinking too rationally. So I need to know what your limits are before we start."

A nervous chill cooled her passion. "Limits? Like…how much weight you can put on a bridge before it collapses?"

"Nothing quite so graphic. But is there any part of your body you don't want touched? Any old injuries I need to be aware of? Any fears you'd rather not face?"

"Well…"

"You need to be honest, Anne."

She blushed and looked away, embarrassed to admit her childhood fear still made her break out in a cold sweat. "I'm afraid of the dark. Not turning the lights out—there's plenty of light from the street outside—but I've never been able to sleep with the covers over my head."

He nodded, accepting her fear. "Anything else? How do you feel about loss of mobility?"

"You mean, like being tied up?" Remembering her fantasy lover's stern demands that she hold still and not move, or the way he'd pinned her in place, her breasts tingled with anticipation. Licking suddenly dry lips, she whispered, "I think I'd like that."

"How about physical stresses? Being upside down, kneeling on the floor, holding a stretched position?"

She frowned. "Why?"

"Just asking." He stroked her cheek again. "I need to know what you're interested in exploring and what you're not, before I can decide how best to please you."

Anne's breath caught. "But you'll make all the decisions, right? You'll be in complete control?"

"Absolutely. For as long as the game continues."

"Good."

They quickly covered Garrett's remaining questions to his satisfaction, then he stood and pulled Anne to her feet.

"Stand absolutely still," he told her. "As if you're a statue. You're not allowed to move."

His words filled her with eager anticipation. What might he do to her while she stood unmoving, unable to escape his torment? Her legs quivered, and she struggled to hide the movement from his view.

"No trembling," he warned. "Like a statue."

Anne took a deep breath and held it, calming herself. Like a statue.

Garrett molded his hands over her hips, caressing her lightly through the soft leather miniskirt. His fingertips slid under the hem of her sweater, and slowly he inched the angora upward, stroking it over her abdomen while his fingers teased their way over her ribs. His thumbs brushed her nipples and she gasped, but he did not linger, bunching the sweater above her breasts. The soft angora tickled the bottom of her chin.

"Close your eyes while I lift this over your head. I'll do it quickly."

Anne smiled, reassured that she would not be in the dark for long. She'd never had a lover who was so attentive to her needs before. Her eyelids fluttered shut.

Garrett pulled the body of the sweater over her head in one quick tug.

"You forgot the sleeves," she reminded him.

He pushed the sweater down behind her, tangling her arms in the angora, trapping them behind her arched back and thrusting her lace-covered chest into prominence. "No, I didn't."

She opened her eyes to see Garrett frowning at her.

"That sounded dangerously like you were trying to tell me what to do," he warned.

"No. No, I wasn't."

"I think you need to be reminded who's in charge here." He hiked her miniskirt up to her waist, grabbed her panties and pantyhose, and jerked them down to her knees, effectively hobbling her.

His hands cupped her ass, playing over the soft contours, rocking her so that she tottered on her high heels. She couldn't move her feet to brace herself, couldn't lift her hands to catch herself if she fell. She was completely at his mercy.

"You're in charge," she said. "You're in control."

Warm liquid trickled down the inside of her thigh, as her body eagerly accepted his mastery of her and hungered for more.

Garrett smiled. "I'm in control. I'm also fully clothed. That needs to change. Undress me."

Anne started to reach for him, but the angora sweater tangled around her arms stopped her. Obviously he wasn't planning on removing the restraint. She nibbled on her lip, considering. "May I turn around?"

"You may." Garrett's smile broadened, and he steadied her hips as she shuffled her hobbled feet, slowly pivoting in a circle.

The sweater pinned her arms together at the upper arm, leaving her hands and lower arms free. She reached blindly behind herself, her questing fingers touching the cotton of his pants. Walking her fingertips to the side, she brushed across the hard ridge of his erection.

Garrett captured her wrists. She yelped in surprise, the noise shifting to a breathy moan when he began rubbing his erection into her cupped palms. He was taking his pleasure from her, any way he wanted it, and she was helpless to resist him. Would he grab her from behind, thrusting into her with no more warning than he'd given when he grabbed her wrists?

Her sex pulsed with anticipation, and she smelled the musky scent of her own readiness.

Releasing her hands, Garrett ordered her, "Unfasten my pants and take my cock out."

"Yes, master." The word slipped out, but once she'd said it, it felt right.

She fumbled for the button at his waistband, and felt him twitch in response. Anne smiled, and purposely made her fingers clumsier, fluttering against his ever-harder erection. But she couldn't tease him for long before he realized what she was doing, so she dutifully unfastened the button and slid down the zipper.

His pants fell from his slim hips, hitting the floor with a muffled whump, and his cock surged forward into her hands. The skin was warm and petal soft, contrasting with the iron hardness within.

"The boxers, too," he reminded her.

"Oh!" Anne felt around the base of his cock, pulling a low growl of pleasure from him. Sure enough, it protruded from the slit in a pair of silk boxers.

She grabbed the waistband and tugged, lifting the elastic past his outthrust erection before lowering the boxers onto his hips. Unlike his pants, the boxers resolutely clung there.

Anne pushed with her fingertips, but only nudged the shorts further down his thighs. This wasn't working.

"You'll have to kneel," he told her. "I'll steady you."

Garrett's strong hands closed around her shoulders, and pressed down. Awkwardly, unable to balance well in her hobbled heels, Anne sank to her knees, pulling his boxers down as she went.

His fingers tightened on her shoulders, and Anne heard the shuffling sound of his shoes being kicked off. She smiled, realizing that now he was leaning against her for balance.

Once the shoes were off, he circled around to stand in front of her. The first two buttons of his collarless shirt were undone, but other than that, from the waist up, he looked much the same as he had during dinner. From the waist down, however, he was completely, gloriously naked — a visual merger of sophistication and animal passion.

Anne admired the light dusting of dark hair that emphasized the strong muscles of his calves and thighs. He stood before her, legs braced slightly apart, as if to counterbalance the weight of his erection, thrusting out from beneath the hem of his shirt.

Garrett stepped forward, closing the distance between them, and buried both of his hands in Anne's hair. Slowly, inexorably, he tilted her head back, until her mouth was level with the head of his cock.

She licked suddenly dry lips and swallowed nervously, as he held her immobile. She stared at his erection, certain it was growing larger before her eyes. And still he continued simply holding her.

The silent waiting stretched her nerves taut. She longed to look up at him, to judge his reaction to their tableau, but she couldn't tear her gaze from the cock waiting less than an inch away from her lips. Her mouth watered, trying to prepare to take that much flesh into her, to lubricate his slide to the back of her throat.

Finally, Garrett moved. His fingers slid through her hair, releasing her, until his palms cradled her jaw. He brushed her lower lip with his thumb, so lightly that under other circumstances she'd question whether he'd really touched her at all. But now, her lips parted eagerly. He stroked her lower lip again, the tip of his thumb slipping inside her mouth.

He skimmed the pad of his thumb across her teeth, then stroked the inside of her lip again.

"So hot. So wet. Is your mouth the only thing this hot and wet, Anne?"

"No." She swallowed, the movement reflexively closing her lips around his thumb and sucking. Now that he'd drawn her attention to the wet heat between her legs, she wanted him there, filling her. If she couldn't have him between her legs, she'd take him in her mouth. Just as long as she could have him, and soon, she didn't care how or where.

Garrett pulled his thumb from her mouth with a soft pop. "I need to get your bed ready. But I don't want you cooling down while I'm away."

Anne's breathing quickened. What was he planning on doing to her bed? And to her, in her bed?

He knelt on the floor in front of her, so they were close to the same height again, and cupped her lace-covered breasts in his hands. Watching her face carefully, he rotated his palms over her nipples, teasing them into hard pebbles. Then he pinched both nipples.

Anne gasped. A tremor rippled through her, and more warmth dribbled down her thigh. She was so hot for him, anything could set her off. Her body was warming up, and judging from her reactions so far, she suspected when she climaxed, the orgasm would rock her world.

Reaching behind her, Garrett unhooked her bra. He stretched the lacy cups over her head, then pushed the straps down her arms, further binding them behind her. Her breasts were now completely bared to his pleasure.

He bent his head and flicked his tongue over first one hard nipple, then the other. Anne let out a shuddering sigh.

"Yes. I know exactly how to keep you hot for me." Garrett chuckled, then rose fluidly to his feet. The breeze he created chilled her damp nipples, and she longed for his hot mouth to close over them again. But she sensed that he was not through with her yet. This alone was not sufficient to keep her primed for his possession.

He crossed the room, disappearing from her view, only to reappear a moment later holding a coil of fine rope. It looked like the decorative braid used to edge pillows.

She trembled with anticipation. Was he going to tie her up now?

Garrett shook out the coil, keeping hold of the ends. It was hard to tell length, since the cord was doubled over, but Anne thought there had to be at least six or eight feet. He dropped the center of the looped cord over her head, pulling it snug against the back of her neck, then letting it fall to the floor before her.

Once more kneeling before her, he knotted the cord so that the knot hung squarely between her breasts. Then slowly, carefully, he began winding the cord under her breasts, around her upper arms, and crossing behind her to wrap the opposite arm, this time passing along the very top of her breasts. He made three passes with the cord, each laid next to the previous one. Then he finished the binding by knotting the cords under her arms, pulling the front and rear cords closer together and compressing the cords against her breasts.

Anne watched the procedure with a wide-eyed mixture of trepidation and delight. She wasn't sure what he was doing to her, but it was really turning her on.

Garrett tested his handiwork, and nodded. "That will keep you thinking of me while I'm busy."

"What…what did you do?"

"The blood is flowing into your breasts, but the cord keeps it from being able to flow back out. So your breasts are growing larger. The skin is stretching to accommodate the swelling, making it more sensitive." He reached over and brushed the rounded top of her breast with his fingertips.

Fire blazed through her. Anne gasped.

"Extremely sensitive," Garrett clarified, brushing butterfly caresses over both breasts.

Anne moaned. Her body twitched uncontrollably, helpless beneath his expert hands. She wasn't sure if she wanted to escape the overwhelmingly intense sensation, or beg for more.

Again, he bent his head and licked each nipple. The stroke of his tongue felt like the harsh scrape of a rasp. Her head tipped back, and a hoarse cry tore from her throat. It was unbearable. She couldn't wait for him to do it again.

Instead, he stood and walked away from her. She heard the muffled thump of the covers being swept off of her bed. Other rustles and thumps followed. As he worked, he spoke to her, ordering her to imagine him fondling her breasts, kissing them, squeezing them, pinching them. Anne trembled, breasts aching, and waited eagerly for him to make his words a reality.

Chapter Four

"All ready," Garrett announced. "On your feet."

"I don't think I can…"

His strong hands grabbed her around the waist from behind, and lifted her to a standing position. Anne wobbled, trying to get her balance when she couldn't move her feet.

Garrett slid down the zipper of her miniskirt slowly, each tooth of the zipper clicking loudly in the silence. Then he pushed the leather over her hips and down her legs.

"I'm kneeling behind you," he told her. "Brace your hands on me."

Confused but willing, Anne searched blindly behind her until her fingers tangled in his thick hair. Pressing her palms against the top of his skull, she leaned back until she felt balanced. "I'm braced."

Garrett's hands caressed her thighs, gliding over her skin, then dipped lower, until his fingers reached the tangle of her stockings and panties hobbling her legs. He shoved the tangle down to her feet.

"Right foot up."

Grateful for his sturdy presence bracing her, Anne obediently lifted her foot. Garrett guided her foot free of the tangle, then set it down and repeated the process with her left foot.

"Stand on your own."

No longer hobbled, Anne spread her legs and stood tall, vividly aware of the inviting picture she presented to the man behind her. Unable to see him, her imagination raced, trying to picture his reaction.

"Turn around."

She turned, and saw him standing between her and the bed. He was still wearing his black shirt, but he'd sheathed his erection in a bright red condom.

Then her attention was captured by what he'd done to her bed. Thick ropes looped over and around each end and side, tied everywhere they crossed, to form a secure frame on the bed.

"Are you going to tie me down?" Anne asked. Her breasts throbbed in their bindings, and she wondered if he would bind the rest of her so that her entire body throbbed, aching for his touch.

"Eventually. First I have to make sure you stayed hot for me, like I told you to."

"I did."

Garrett picked up an electric-blue, fluffy ostrich feather he'd left on the bed. Holding it just above her breasts, he tipped it so that the fine hairs on the edge of the feather stroked her tender skin.

Anne gasped, her eyes going wide. She shouldn't have been able to feel such a light touch. It certainly shouldn't have felt like fingers of fire stroking her.

Then he drew the fluffy feather over the mound of her breast and tickled her nipple. Anne groaned, unable to believe a feather could feel so hard and firm. When he stroked her other breast with his fingernails, she clenched her hands into fists and whimpered. She wasn't sure how to describe what she was feeling. It wasn't pain, and it wasn't pleasure. It was raw sexual arousal, and she wanted more.

"Oh, very good," Garrett purred. He circled behind her and freed her arms from her sweater and bra, tossing the clothing to the floor. Then he turned Anne so that she could see her reflection in the mirror.

"Look at yourself. See how hot you are for me. How badly you want me."

Anne saw her face first. Her lips were dark red with arousal, and her cheeks were flushed. Her hair, normally styled to perfection, fluffed around her head in rumpled disarray, as if they'd already been romping between the sheets.

Then her gaze shifted lower, to her bound and straining breasts.

"Dear God, they're huge!"

Garrett chuckled from behind her as he began untying the cord. "Like two ripe melons. And you know what we do with melons. Pluck them."

He reached around her and tugged both her nipples.

Anne cried out at the sudden pain, moaning as waves of pleasure followed. She panted, gasping for breath in short, sharp bursts. All her awareness focused on Garrett's hands on her breasts, tugging, rolling, and squeezing the sensitive, swollen flesh. Just when she thought she could take no more, his hands would lift, leaving her cold and longing for his touch, before he began another agonizing assault. She strained toward a release that hovered tantalizingly just out of reach.

"Please, Garrett. Please."

"No." He lifted his hands and stepped away from her. "I decide when you've had enough, and when you can come. You haven't had enough yet."

Anne whined, a low animal noise from deep in her throat. She wanted more. God, how she wanted more! But she wasn't sure she could take the tension.

Shivering from the waves of pleasure still rippling through her, she followed meekly when Garrett took her hand and led her to the bed.

"Lie down on your back."

She did as he commanded, opening her legs wide in invitation. But he ignored the mute plea, instead giving his attention to the wide suede bands he was buckling around her wrists and ankles. He threaded spring clips through the metal rings on the cuffs, and clipped her wrists and ankles to loops in the ropes framing her bed.

Anne's arms stretched to the sides, and her legs were spread as wide as possible, leaving her naked and completely vulnerable to anything Garrett wanted to do to her. She was under his complete control, and had never felt so free.

Garrett picked up the discarded feather, and stroked it lightly over her still swollen breasts. Liquid fire flowed from her chest to her open, hungry sex.

Anne moaned and arched her back, eager for more.

Garrett pulled the feather away. "No-no, my dear, sweet slave. You must lie completely still. You may not move, and you may not come, until I give you permission."

"Yes, master," she whispered.

"Such a good, obedient slave." He rewarded her with a soft stroke over the other breast.

Anne's breath left her on a shaky sigh.

Garrett continued torturing her breasts with the feather, stopping every time she began building toward a climax. Then he would stroke the feather softly over her cheeks, soothing her, or distract her by suddenly tickling her toes. He brushed the soft tip of the feather over her arms and legs, warming her entire body, and fluttered it against the damp skin of her inner thighs. She moaned, liquid flowing between her legs as he drove her to a fever pitch again and again, but always stopping just short of the edge. Her world narrowed to a single focus, the heat that leaped from his slightest touch, feeding the roaring need that threatened to consume her utterly.

When he abandoned his toys of torment to lie between her legs, she felt like he'd finally come home to where he belonged. His sheathed erection slid smoothly inside her flowing channel. Anne moaned and whimpered, unable to form coherent words to tell him how much joy his presence inside her gave to her. He seemed to understand, moving slowly in and out.

Then he rose to his knees, changing the angle of his thrusts, scraping across her tender opening with each pump of his hips. She clutched the ropes beside her wrists, fighting to retain control. She must not come. He had told her not to come.

Garrett leaned down and kissed the damp skin beside each of her eyes, licking her tears away.

"Now, my darling slave, this time you may come."

Anne shivered, trembling with anticipation as he began moving faster, sliding in and out of her with more force. The haze of passion claimed her again, building to a peak, but this time she knew he would send her flying from the heights.

His hands seemed to touch her everywhere, stroking and caressing as he thrust into her, hard and fast. The combination of tenderness and urgency threatened to drive her mad, spiraling her higher and higher. Then he grabbed her hips and thrust deeper than before, until she could feel his balls against her skin, and he rocked within her.

Anne gasped and panted, reaching, reaching, reaching...and howled as her release burst through her, shaking her to every atom of her being.

Garrett came a moment later, her convulsions seizing him and milking every drop from his rigid cock. And still the aftershocks shuddered through her, longer and deeper than any she'd ever experienced. Freed from her body, her mind spun away, drifting in a timeless haze where nothing existed but pleasure, fulfillment, and the soul-deep knowledge that this was how sex was meant to be.

Anne opened her eyes to see a well-formed chest beneath her cheek. She blinked, and gradually became aware that she was lying cuddled in Garrett's arms, their legs entwined and her head pillowed upon his chest. At some point he'd untied her and removed the last of his clothing, as well as retrieved the bedclothes from the floor.

He was stroking her hair, lightly, rhythmically. She closed her eyes and sighed, nestling deeper into his embrace.

"Hey, sleepyhead," he teased. "The game's over. You can say something now."

"No. Can't," Anne whispered, her thick tongue struggling to form the words. "Tired. Sleep."

"Poor Anne. Tonight was almost too much for you."

She made an inarticulate sound of protest, and Garrett chuckled, gently stroking her cheek.

"I said, 'almost'." Abruptly his hand stilled, and the humor faded from his voice. "Would you like me to leave so you can get some sleep?"

"No! No go." Anne clutched his chest, fisting her fingers in the light dusting of hairs. "Stay."

Garrett winced, and carefully pried her fingers from their grip on his chest hairs. "All right. I'll stay."

Smoothing her hand over his warm chest, Anne closed her eyes. He wouldn't be able to stay forever. He'd made that abundantly clear. But for the moment, life was perfect.

* * * * *

Anne woke, still cuddled in Garrett's arms. His deep, even breathing indicated he was still asleep, so she took advantage of the opportunity to study him.

His dark hair looked delightfully tousled, and a hint of morning beard shadowed his jaw. She smiled, suspecting that the reason it was so faint was that he'd taken the trouble to shave last night before their date. It seemed just the sort of considerate thing he'd do.

She ran her fingers lightly over his shoulder and down his well-defined chest, caressing him the way she hadn't been able to last night. Last night. Anne's smile broadened, remembering what she'd done instead, and what he'd done to her.

"Good morning. And from that smile, a very good morning it must be, too." Garrett grinned sleepily up at her.

"Oh, I'm sorry. I didn't mean to wake you."

"I wasn't really asleep. I was just too comfortable to move." His eyelids drifted closed, but his hand at her hip began stroking and caressing her with small, soft circles.

They lay together quietly, gently caressing each other, while their hearts and lungs moved in time to a single, slow beat. Finally, Anne spoke.

"Last night was the most phenomenal sex I've ever had. Is it always like that?"

"You mean, does playing the game while you make love always feel like someone's opened the top of your head and filled your brain with Pop Rocks?"

Anne giggled at his description, but it did match the fizzing fireworks she'd experienced. "Yes."

"No."

He rolled over, pinning her beneath him. She instantly stilled, her entire body humming with eager anticipation as she waited for his next move. Straddling her hips so that his rapidly firming erection pressed against her stomach, he cupped his hands around her breasts, teasing her nipples into hard pebbles. Anne closed her eyes and moaned, waves of desire rippling outward from his touch.

"No," Garrett repeated. "I've never found anyone so responsive before."

"It's Saturday," she whispered. "I don't have anywhere I have to be."

"We have time." He rotated his hands around her breasts, pressing lightly, and wrung another moan from her. "But I'm not interested in another elaborate scene. I just want to take you now."

She felt the telltale warmth between her legs, her body remembering all he'd done to her last night and ready for him to do it again. "Take me as hard and as fast as you want."

Garrett groaned, his fingers tightening on her breasts. "You say the sweetest things. Okay."

He slid off of her, sweeping back the covers as he did so. Leaning past her, he reached beneath his pillow and retrieved a condom.

"Your version of sleeping with a loaded weapon beneath your pillow?" Anne asked.

"My weapon is fully loaded," he assured her. "This ensures it won't go off unexpectedly."

"Do you want me to put it on you?"

"You know, it's possible to hold an opened condom in your mouth, so that as the cock slides between your lips, you unroll the condom over it."

She swallowed, her mind filled with images of taking him in her mouth. "Is that what you want?"

"No, I only have the one here, and that trick takes a lot of practice. We can work on it later."

He ripped open the package and unrolled the condom, bright green this time, over his erection.

Then he rose to his knees, and pointed at the bed in front of him.

"Kneel here, facing the headboard."

Anne scrambled to her knees in front of him, her legs spread so that her calves bracketed his. She could feel the heat of his body behind her, but could not see him. For the first time in her life, she understood why people wanted mirrors above their beds.

Garrett's hands settled on her hips, holding her where he wanted her. She trembled with anticipation, but he did not immediately begin thrusting into her.

"Lean forward. Cross your arms and rest them on the bed, then cushion your head on your arms."

Not quite sure what he was asking, she went to her hands and knees. Then to her elbows. Finally, she rested her forehead on her crossed arms.

"This is incredibly uncomfortable."

Garrett's hands on her hips stilled. "Uncomfortable, painful? Or uncomfortable, awkward and humiliating?"

Anne hesitated. Garrett would never do something that would hurt her. All she had to do was say that this position caused her pain, that the tensions of her job made the muscles of her neck and back too tight to bend this way. Except it wouldn't be true. And she sensed that lying to him about her feelings would destroy whatever mutual trust was required to play the game.

"No, not painful, just...scary."

"Is it too much like being in the dark?"

Anne let out a relieved sigh. That was it exactly. "Yes. I can't see with my face against the bed."

"Hmm. Let me think." His fingers tapped idly against her hip, then his warm presence vanished from behind her. A moment later, something soft pressed against the front of her forearms.

"What's that?"

"Pillows. Lift up."

She moved back to her hands and knees, watching as Garrett placed the pillows where her folded arms had been. He pressed the heel of his hand into the soft down, checking how far it sank.

"Okay. Try it now."

Knowing the position she was ultimately striving for this time, Anne folded her arms and rested them on the pillows, then lowered her forehead onto her arms. Her eyes were a good inch and a half above the mattress now, allowing plenty of light. She was so relieved, she didn't care that her ass was sticking up in the air exposing her sex to the world.

"Much better," she assured him.

"Good." He circled back around her, once again kneeling between her spread legs. "Now stay like that, lifted and spread for my pleasure."

His hands stroked her ass, and Anne sighed with delight. Then he reached between her legs, sliding his fingers between her folds. She gasped, jerking at the unexpectedly intimate caress.

Garrett lightly swatted her ass, getting her attention. "No. You're not allowed to move. I can see we'll have to practice this."

His fingers slid up and down her folds, questing for the hot nub of swollen flesh by her clitoris. He brushed the tight bud, and she shuddered, letting out a shaky moan. Target acquired, Garrett ruthlessly tortured her, flicking his fingers back and forth over the sensitive skin. Every time she tried to move with him, he swatted her ass again, reminding her that she was supposed to stay still. Finally, she managed to keep her hips from moving by clenching the pillows in her fists. Every flick of Garrett's fingers drove a harsh gasp from her throat, but the rest of her stayed immobile.

He took his hands away, and Anne panted like a marathon runner. Then his lips closed over her tender flesh, sucking on her and scraping the sensitive skin with his teeth. She whimpered, legs trembling, her knuckles aching from her death grip on the pillows. His thumbs, already slick with her fluids, parted her folds, testing her readiness to take him.

Her body clenched around his thumbs, eager and demanding, and Garrett chuckled, the soft exhalations tickling and teasing her almost beyond endurance.

As if recognizing that he'd driven her as far as he could before pushing her over the edge, he shifted his position, once again kneeling close behind her. The tip of his erection teased her wide-open entrance and she moaned. Deep contractions coursed through her as her body attempted to capture and claim the eagerly welcomed intruder. Then Garrett pushed inside her, sheathing himself in one long, fluid thrust.

Grabbing her by the hips, he rocked against her, pulling her toward him with each deep thrust and pushing her away as he withdrew. He moved faster, entering her harder, grunting each time he slammed into her. Soon she was grunting with him, harsh animal noises ripped from some primal place within her.

The pace built, faster and harder, until she was flying in a haze of passion. Reaching, over and over again, for a prize just out of her grasp. Then Garrett's fingers slipped between their damp bodies, searching for the swollen bud still aching from his previous assault.

His fingers brushed her swollen flesh, and Anne screamed, a powerful orgasm tearing through her. With a triumphant shout, Garrett burst in his own release.

Chapter Five

Anne retained enough sense of her surroundings to hear Garrett's muttered, "Game Over," and recognize the shifting mattress and sounds of running water that meant he was cleaning up. He returned with a warm washcloth for her.

"Anne? Do you want to wash up, or would you like me to do it for you?"

"Mmm. You."

He chuckled. "Lost your verbal skills again, I see. I guess that means you enjoyed it."

"Oh, yeah."

Kneeling beside her, Garrett gently stroked the washcloth over her sensitive skin. She moaned, flashes of ecstasy dancing along her overwrought nerves. But his slow, soft touch soothed and calmed her rather than sparking another spiral of passion.

She lay sprawled on her back, drifting in a pleasant cloud of peace and contentment as he cared for her. Too soon, he was done.

"May I use your shower? You can take a little nap while I get ready."

Anne nodded, visions of lathering Garrett's hot, wet body with cascades of soap bubbles threatening to destroy her peace. "We could shower together."

"Soaping each other up in the hot steam? We'd never finish the shower. And as soon as your endorphins go back to normal, I'm betting you'll find you're too sore to make love again. That last time was pretty intense."

Anne smiled, recalling the total and complete release he'd given her. She was still smiling when he returned from the bathroom, showered, shaved, and dressed in clean clothes. Then she noticed that he was carrying his black leather duffel bag.

"Going somewhere?"

"I need to get going. I've got a luncheon meeting."

"But it's Saturday."

"Of course. The senior partners wouldn't dare take me away from the markets for over an hour during trading hours." He flashed a sharp grin. "It could wind up being an unexpectedly expensive lunch."

Anne's happy mood vanished, dispelled by the reminder of Garrett's looming partnership, and move to Europe. "Will I see you again?"

"I'd like that. What are you doing tomorrow night?"

She considered her calendar. Mondays started early in the office, as they gathered to discuss their competitors' campaigns that had rolled during the weekend, and analyze preliminary results of their own campaigns. As a result, she normally kept Sunday nights free.

"I'm free."

"Great. Why don't we get together again?"

"Sure. When and where?"

"Ten o'clock? I know a great nightclub I'm sure you'd enjoy."

Anne winced. They wouldn't get back until at least midnight, and she had to be up at four. "Let's make it earlier. I've got an early morning Monday. How's your Sunday afternoon? We could go to a museum, or the zoo."

Garrett thought for a moment. "The zoo sounds like fun. Pick you up at four?"

"Four o'clock."

He leaned down and gave her a thorough kiss. When he broke it off, she blinked in passion-glazed confusion.

"Why…?"

"Just a promise of things to come. I don't want you to forget about me."

Anne groaned. As if she could forget the most phenomenal sex she'd ever experienced. Her mouth went dry as all of her body's moisture seemed to pool between her legs. She was hot for him now, and knowing she'd have to wait a full day only made her want him more.

Garrett just laughed, and tweaked her nipple lightly before turning and leaving her bedroom. She heard the front door open and close a moment later, followed by the low, throaty roar of his car's engine.

Dragging herself out of the rumpled bed, Anne staggered into the bathroom. She needed a cold shower.

* * * * *

She met Sarah for lunch, a lighter version of the birthday meal Anne had originally been promised. Showing amazing self-restraint, Sarah actually waited until Anne sat down and picked up her menu before pouncing.

"So? How was the date? Was he everything you'd hoped for?"

Anne closed her eyes and sighed. "More than I dreamed of."

Sarah squealed, causing heads to turn throughout the small restaurant. The jaded diners quickly went back to their own meals, ignoring the girls.

"You got laid! I knew that's what you needed."

"No way, Sarah. Getting laid is ten minutes of grunting followed by getting dressed and going home. This was...I don't know how to describe it. Garrett was like an artist, and making love was his piece of performance art. I've never felt anything like it. It was beyond orgasmic."

"Wow," Sarah breathed, staring at her in rapt fascination. "I should've kept him for myself and bought you a sweater for your birthday. Well, at least I've still got his number."

"Hands off, sister! He's mine. We're going out again tomorrow."

"Another dinner, followed by performance art sex?" Sarah sipped her lemon water, and tried to look blasé.

"No. He's taking me to the zoo."

Sarah sprayed water over the table, coughing and choking. Finally, she recovered enough to gasp, "The zoo? Tell me you're not serious. That's for married couples with little kids, not hot dates."

Anne just smiled and turned her attention to her menu.

"What?" Sarah asked. "Come on, Anne. You can't just grin like that and not say anything.

"I think he might be planning on using it for inspiration." Anne slapped her menu on the damp table, cutting off Sarah's comment. "Plus it will give us a chance to see how compatible we are when we're not playing games or making love."

"Didn't you do that at dinner?"

"No. Dinner was one long tease, leading up to my asking him to stay the night."

"He stayed the night? Girl, you have got it bad."

"You don't know the half of it. All I can think about is how we made love, and I get hot all over again every time I remember. By the time he comes to pick me up on Sunday, I may just rip his clothes off and jump him in the foyer."

Except she knew that she wouldn't. She'd be demure and docile, doing whatever he commanded, the agonizing tension between what she wanted and what he allowed her to do stoking the fires of her passion higher and hotter, until she exploded in another mind-numbing orgasm. Her nipples hardened and her panties grew damp, anticipating her climax to come.

"I don't think I've ever seen you so worked up about a guy. Does he feel the same way?"

"He said he'd never had a partner so responsive as I was."

"Sounds like you hit the jackpot on this one."

"I think I did. Except…"

"Except what?"

Anne shrugged, dismissing her concern as unimportant.

"No, go on. What was it except for? It must've been important or you wouldn't have mentioned it at all."

"There's no future in the relationship. Even now, he's off meeting with his boss to discuss a transfer to London. What if I really fall for him?"

Sarah chewed on her straw, considering. "When is he leaving?"

"Two months, I think."

"That's plenty of time for an affair to run its course. Keep the sex hot and heavy, but keep your emotions light and noncommittal, and you'll be fine."

Anne raised her water glass and clinked the rim against Sarah's. "To hot and heavy sex with no emotional commitment."

She was a modern woman. She could handle this. So what if she wanted more? Life was all about compromise. Just yesterday, she'd never dreamed she'd find a lover who made her feel the way Garrett did. She should be thankful for what she got, and enjoy the good times for as long as they lasted.

Resolving to forget about the future, and live in the moment, Anne shelved all thoughts of Garrett, and turned her full attention to ordering lunch.

* * * * *

Garrett arrived promptly at four o'clock Sunday afternoon for their date, dressed casually in black jeans and an olive polo shirt. His heated gaze devoured Anne in her loose jeans and cotton sweater as if she'd still been wearing the clinging miniskirt and angora.

"Ready?" he asked.

"Let's go." She left the house before she could change her mind and invite him inside for an afternoon of passionate sex. The whole point of today's date was to get to know Garret's heart and mind as well as his body, and she'd never do that in bed.

He helped her into his car, pulling out the seatbelt for her but not reaching across to fasten it. "No games today."

"No games," she agreed. "At least, not at the zoo."

"You do say the sweetest things."

His hand did brush her jean-clad leg once during the drive to the zoo, but it was truly accidental, when an overzealous cabby cut them off and Garrett had to unexpectedly downshift.

"What do you want to see first?" she asked.

"They should be starting to feed the animals soon. If there's a schedule of feeding times, we can follow that."

Anne nodded. "Sounds good. Let's be sure to visit the Jungle World exhibit, though. The cubs are supposed to be out now."

"We'll hit that first, then."

Their plans made, they avoided the crowds milling aimlessly around the main gate of the zoo, driving deeper inside to the small auxiliary parking lot that brought them out right at Jungle World.

While most of the cats were in a realistic bit of savannah-like habitat to the east, hemmed in by the observation monorail, the nursing mothers were in regular cages where the zookeepers could keep an eye on them and their babies. Anne and Garrett joined the throng of people admiring the tiger and lion cubs.

"They're so cute," Anne cooed.

"Hard to believe those tiny bundles of fluff are going to grow up into six hundred pound predators capable of bringing down anything from a zebra to a rhinoceros."

The mother tiger, perturbed by the gawking crowd, let loose a full-throated, rumbling roar. A moment later, her cub echoed her with a tiny, "Mow!"

She nosed the little ball of fur, and once more voiced her deep roar. He tried again, this time managing a slightly fiercer, "Row!"

Anne laughed and clapped her hands. "Isn't that sweet? She's teaching her baby to roar."

"Adorable," Garrett agreed, smiling. But he was looking at her rather than the tigers.

It seemed natural for Garrett to take Anne's hand to lead her away from the tigers, and her fingers twined easily with his. They wandered hand in hand through the rest of the zoo, watching the lazy gorillas come to life as their food arrived, and admiring the strength and beauty of a herd of zebras, spooked into a stampede by some invisible signal. Garrett bought them both hot dogs and sodas, so they could feed themselves, too. And as they walked, they talked. Which animals did they most admire? Which would they like to be reincarnated as?

"They look bored," Anne announced, studying the pythons through the glass windows of the World of Reptiles.

"I don't think they can look excited. Hungry or bored are pretty much their only expressions."

"If I were a zoo animal, I'd be bored."

Garrett looked at her with interest. "Would you trade a long life of peace and well-being in a zoo for a short, dangerous life in the wild?"

"No question. I'd go for the excitement. Even if the life were shorter, it would be more worth living. How about you?"

"The wild. I'd want my freedom."

Anne nodded, and moved to look at the next snake. She couldn't allow herself to forget, Garrett would be free of her in two months. They seemed so in tune with each other, sometimes it felt like she'd known him forever, and would go on knowing him forever. But that was as much a fantasy as her imaginary lover had been.

Then she registered what it was she was looking at. "Eww, gross! That snake has half a mouse hanging out of his mouth!"

Garrett slid his arm around her, comforting her distress. "Snakes have to eat, too."

"But he's not eating it. He's just sitting there, with it half…oh, God, did the mouse's tail just move?"

Garrett turned her away from the snake. "Don't worry, the mouse is dead. The tail must have just brushed a twig or something when the snake swallowed a bit more of it."

Anne shuddered, grateful for Garrett's explanation even if it was a lie. "I think I've had enough of the zoo. Let's go home."

He led her past the big cats again on their way out of the zoo, pausing long enough for the tiger cub's small roars to cheer her. Then they were in the car and driving toward her brownstone.

"I have to get up early," she told him as the BMW pulled up outside her home. "I mean really early. Four o'clock. So you can't spend the night. But if you'd like to come in for a few hours, that's okay."

"Just okay?" Garrett teased.

"That would be great," she corrected herself. "And we can play another game."

Garrett stroked her cheek lightly with one finger. Anne closed her eyes and tilted her head, exulting in his gently possessive touch.

"You'd like that, wouldn't you?" he asked.

"Oh, yes," she breathed. "I've been thinking about our last date ever since you left."

"Then by all means, let the games begin."

Chapter Six

Garrett retrieved the familiar black leather duffel bag from his car's trunk, and followed her into the brownstone. She headed for her bedroom, but his light touch on her arm stopped her.

"We both smell like zoo. I think now is a good time to take you up on your offer to share a shower."

Anne eagerly turned toward the bathroom instead. "Whatever you say, master."

As he followed her down the hall, he asked, "How do you feel after yesterday's sex? Any soreness?"

"A little," she admitted, then worried he'd feel he had to skip having sex with her now. "But it was nothing much. Just enough to remind me of how good it felt."

He nodded. "We'll be careful today."

Garrett dropped his bag in the hall, and they crowded into the green and white tiled bathroom. He stripped off his own clothing, while Anne waited patiently for instruction, then stripped off hers. His hands skimmed lightly over her body, warming and arousing her. Then he pointed to the tub enclosure.

"In you go."

She stepped in, backing toward the spigot so he'd have plenty of room. After some awkward maneuvering, they managed to adjust the water temperature and turn on the shower, so that it cascaded over them both in a warm flow.

Garrett handed her the soap, then turned to face the far wall. Anne's Saturday morning daydream was coming true. She quickly worked up a thick lather, and began soaping his muscled back. Bracing his hands on the tile, he bent his head, relaxing under her ministrations.

"How much hot water do you have?"

"Twenty minutes."

"Damn. We'll have to make this quick."

He seemed in no hurry to move, however, so Anne pressed against him, using her own body to rub the soap against his, and reached around him to lather his front. Her hands stroked his well-defined chest, then fluttered down over his ribs in a soapy caress. Garrett sucked in a quick breath. Her hands closed over his erection, lathering the length of it with long, sure strokes.

Garrett groaned. "That's enough, or I'll come right here. It's your turn now."

Anne handed over the soap, then turned away from him, bracing her hands against the wall as he had done and letting the shower spray beat against her bent head. His wet hands trailed soap suds over her back and shoulders, then across her breasts. He fondled them a moment, his fingers slipping over and around her soap-slicked nipples, and she released her breath in a shaky sigh.

He glided the soap between her legs, and then lathered her ass. In the warm, sudsy water, his fingers slid up and down the cleft, then one finger slipped inside her ass.

Anne gasped, sucking in a mouthful of wet air. His finger made small, soapy circles as her ass muscles clenched and spasmed around him. She moaned, hoping he'd replace his finger with his hard cock.

Instead, Garrett backed away. "Time to rinse off."

They washed the clinging soap suds away, then turned off the water and stepped out of the tub. Garrett toweled her off, the brisk chafing further arousing her, and Anne did her best to return the favor while drying him. His low groan and muffled oath as the towel rubbed his erection indicated she succeeded.

They headed for the bedroom, Garrett grabbing the duffel bag as they passed. He handed her a lacy black thong in a sealed pouch.

"Here, put this on."

The underwear was little more than an elasticized lace waistband, with another band of lace connecting them. She stepped into the panties. As she pulled them up, the lace slid between her legs, slipping between her outer folds to tease her already aroused sex, at the same time tucking into the cleft in her ass, reminding her of Garrett's recent soapy exploration.

He placed the now-familiar cuffs around her wrists and ankles, and Anne felt the thong growing wet with her excitement. As Garrett tightened the cuffs, he talked to her, directing her to imagine the wet lace between her legs was his cock, pressing against her. Then he told her to kneel, legs spread, on the floor, and grab her ankles. Anne gasped as the thong slid further between her hot folds of flesh.

Garrett clipped her wrist and ankle cuffs together on each side, then fastened them to eyes set at each end of a thick wooden dowel. She could not rise from her kneeling position, and could not close her legs. She was completely at his mercy. Hot fluid trickled down the inside of one leg.

Behind her, Garrett rummaged in his duffel bag. She heard the rip of a condom packet, and pictured him sheathing his erection in the bright plumage of his colored condoms. Then she heard something thick squirting out.

"A little lubrication," he explained.

Anne knew better than to contradict or correct him during the game, but now she was confused. "I'm already dripping wet for you."

"True. But that's not where this is going."

Garrett knelt behind her, his fingers slipping beneath the damp lace of the thong and her ass. She trembled, realizing what he intended.

Then the slick, lubricated condom pressed against the opening of her ass. Too small to be his cock, too thick to be his finger, she wasn't sure what the condom covered. Whatever it was, Garrett was sliding it slowly into her ass.

Her muscles clenched again, as they had in the shower, and she moaned. The hard, thick whatever-it-was felt even better than Garrett's soapy finger had.

Patiently, waiting for her muscles to relax and expand, Garrett inched the thing into her ass. Twice, a wave of pleasure crested over her, leaving her gasping and half-blind, but he denied her the release of an orgasm. She knew if he began pumping the thing in and out of her ass, she'd come in an instant, but that wasn't his plan. When it was fully sheathed, he tugged the lace thong back into place, holding the thing inside her.

He cupped her ass, then began rotating his palms on the globes, stretching and loosening her muscles around the thing. Anne trembled, more hot fluid rolling down her leg, and picked up his rhythm, clenching and releasing her muscles. The wet lace teased her hungry sex with every contraction, but that opening remained empty. Tears of frustration leaked from the corners of her eyes.

"Good." Garrett stood and walked around in front of her. His erection jutted proudly before him. He frowned, and wiped the tears from her cheek. "Is there a problem, Anne?"

"No, master," she gasped.

"Are you crying because the butt plug feels so good inside you?"

"I'm crying because you're not inside me."

"We can fix that." He buried his hands in her hair, holding her head steady. Anticipating his intent, Anne opened her mouth. His hard, hot cock slipped between her lips. "If you want me inside you, you'll have to show me how much you want me."

As he slowly invaded her mouth with his cock, as slowly as he'd entered her ass with the butt plug, Anne sucked with enthusiasm. Her tongue fondled the head of his cock, licking the sensitive slit at the tip. Garrett groaned, his fingers tightening in her hair.

She redoubled her efforts, sucking and tonguing him. He began sliding his shaft in and out of her mouth, although the head always remained in the wet warmth of her mouth. Gently, he tilted her head backward, allowing his thrusts to go deeper, sliding all the way to the back of her throat.

Her confused senses combined the aching pressure of the butt plug with the cock sliding in and out of her mouth, until she felt each of his thrusts filling her ass as well as her throat. She tasted a salty sweetness on the tip of his cock, then he pulled himself from her mouth with a groan and took a step backward. A moment later, hot come shot from his swollen cock, splashing over her breasts and shoulders.

Garrett swayed on his feet, then took a deep breath.

"Oh, yeah. You want me, all right."

Going to one knee on the floor beside her, he reached one arm beneath her thighs, and another across her back. He lifted her, still bound, and placed her on her bed. Taking a pair of surgical scissors from his bag, he cut through the lace thong, exposing her sex. Then he lay down on the bed, put his head between her legs, and took her with his mouth and tongue.

Anne came almost instantly, the orgasm shuddering through her, quickly followed by a second, triggered by the butt plug still clenched tightly in her ass, and Garrett's nimble tongue. Shaking from the force of her passion, the butt plug continued to tease her. When Garrett shifted to suck on the swollen bud of her clitoris, she screamed, and an unbelievable third orgasm ripped through her. Then she was floating in a happy world of complete and total sexual surrender, and felt nothing more.

When she awoke, her bindings were gone, her ass was empty, and Garrett had cleaned up the mess of their lovemaking. Somehow, he'd also gotten both of them under the covers.

"Wow," she whispered.

"You've been out for nearly an hour," he told her. "I was getting concerned that you'd gone to sleep for the night, and I couldn't remember what time you said you needed to be up tomorrow."

"Four."

He whistled softly. "That is early. Is your alarm set?"

Anne blinked, thought, then shook her head. "Alarm two."

Garrett leaned over and inspected her alarm clock. After a moment, he slid the switch on the side from Alarm One to Alarm Two, and slid another switch from Off to Alarm.

"All set. You can go to sleep now. I'll let myself out."

"No. Stay."

He chuckled and brushed her hair out of her eyes. "You can't even talk straight, let alone think straight. You said earlier, when you were still coherent, that I couldn't stay the night, so I won't stay. I only waited this long so you wouldn't wake up and find me gone."

Garrett climbed out of the bed, and kissed her softly on the lips.

"I'll call you tomorrow. Good night. Sleep well."

She watched him pick up his bag and walk down the hall, then heard him getting dressed in the bathroom. A short time later, she heard the front door open and shut, followed by the roar of his car.

Anne huddled beneath the suddenly cold covers. He wouldn't stay. Not tonight, and not long-term. No matter how phenomenal the sex between them was, she couldn't forget that in two months' time, he'd be moving to London.

* * * * *

Anne wanted to spend every minute of those two months with Garrett, but her business consumed most of her days and evenings. Their schedules didn't allow them to meet again until the next Friday, although this time they had the entire weekend together.

She thought she might resent her business, for taking her time away from Garrett, but just the opposite seemed to have occurred. Spending much of the weekend in bed as his willing and obedient slave made her relaxed and accepting of the constant decisions she was called upon to make during the work week. For the first time in months, she didn't begrudge her level of involvement in running her advertising agency. Her employees seemed to pick up on her more relaxed attitude, and the office became a perceptibly more pleasant environment.

By their third weekend together, she knew that their affair would not run its course in two months. She could easily picture herself with Garrett forever. She'd caught herself thinking about how they would spend the Thanksgiving and Christmas holidays, until she remembered he'd be long gone by then.

Ever attuned to her moods, Garrett asked her what was bothering her as they walked along the riverfront park.

"I'm thinking about what will happen after you leave in five weeks."

He stared at the distant skyline across the river, but Anne doubted he saw any of the buildings. "I've been thinking about that, too. I wish I'd met you six months ago."

"If wishes were fishes…"

Garrett laughed. "Yes, I know. Not a very productive thought. But what can we do? You can't leave your agency. And I have to go to London."

Anne stepped closer and wrapped herself in his warm embrace. "We can't solve it. So let's not think about it. Let's just enjoy our time together."

He held her close, his hands stroking up and down her back, warming her skin through the thin cotton of her sweater. "I'm meeting with three of the senior partners for dinner Tuesday night to finalize the terms of the London deal. I might be able to postpone it, push the move back a month or two."

Anne shook her head. "No. I know how businesses work. Give them any reason to think there's something more important to you than their company, and you're off the fast track for good. You have to go, Garrett."

"Well, it will only be for two years. Then I'll be back."

She could barely stand the wait from Sunday to Friday, she was so eager to see him each weekend. Anne didn't know how she'd manage to wait for two years.

"Take me home now, please," Anne whispered. "I want to make love."

Chapter Seven

Garrett called Anne at work on Wednesday. "Friday is our one-month anniversary. Would you like to celebrate with dinner at Paloma's?"

"Can we play the game in public again?"

"Of course."

"Then I would love to go back to Paloma's."

She spent the rest of the week in a state of eager anticipation. Would it be as good as it had been the first time, now that she knew what to expect? Or would it be even better?

Anne dressed carefully for the special evening. The same black leather micro-miniskirt she'd worn the first time, which Garrett had delighted in caressing her through and reaching under. A lacy black sweater with marabou trim, to remind him of the lacy thong he'd given her to wear, and the feather he'd tortured her with on more than one occasion. Her black stockings were patterned with tiny interlocking circles, which she thought looked like the cuffs he bound about her wrists and ankles.

When Garrett saw her, his breath caught in his throat. Kicking the brownstone's door closed, he pinned her against the wall of the foyer, his hands caressing her hips then slipping under her skirt to caress her ass while he pressed hot kisses along the swell of her breasts, his breath fluttering the feather trim of her sweater in a teasing caress.

"You are so gorgeous. I want to take you right here, right now."

He nudged her legs apart, and pressed his hips to hers so that she could feel the strength of his erection against her pulsing flesh.

"Whatever you desire, master. I am yours, completely."

Garrett leaned back to look into her eyes, although his hands continued stroking and kneading her ass. "Will you be? My slave, completely? No games now."

Anne blinked, not sure what he was asking. "I don't understand your question."

Reluctantly, he released her and stepped back, then took a deep breath. Reaching into his jacket pocket, he withdrew a long, flat jeweler's box. He snapped it open, revealing an intricate gold choker of interlocking links, with a bead of banded agate dropping from the center.

"In ancient Roman days, slaves were identified by the collars they wore. Will you wear my collar, Anne? Will you show the world that you are my slave?"

A rush of warmth and contentment filled her. No matter how far away he traveled, or how long he was away, he would always return to her. She was his chosen slave.

"Always and forever," she whispered. "Will you put it on me now?"

Garrett lifted the necklace from the box. "Turn around."

Anne turned and faced the wall, reaching back to lift her hair off of her neck. The heavy gold pulled snugly around her throat as he fastened the clasp, then slid down to settle at the base of her neck.

She turned again to face him, twining her arms around Garrett's broad back, beaming with delight. "It feels like a permanent caress, like the weight of your hands will always be resting on my shoulders."

"This way, I'll always be with you, touching you, holding you, even when I'm away." He reached out and flicked the agate bead with the tip of one finger. "And agate is supposed to be a strong gemstone, imparting health, vitality, and endurance. You'll need that for when I'm here."

Anne held her breath, unwilling to vocalize the hope beating in her chest. Finally, she whispered, "When will you be here?"

"Every other weekend, my dear, darling slave."

A shout of delight escaped her lips, and she threw herself at him, wrapping her legs around his waist and her arms around his neck while she covered his face with happy kisses. Garrett staggered, then caught his balance against the far wall, and wrapped his arms around her waist, holding her tight. His lips caught and captured hers, returning her kisses with mind-drugging interest. Soon she was weak with need, clinging to him as she rubbed her aching breasts against his chest, and he rocked his hard cock against the damp barrier of her panties.

He groaned. "My protection's in the car, and I don't want to wait. Take me in your mouth, Anne. Make love to me now."

He released her, standing her on trembling legs. She quickly unfastened his belt, unzipped his pants, and pushed pants and boxers to the floor. His erection sprung forth, hot and hard and already beading at the tip.

Anne dropped to her knees on the cold floor of the foyer, reveling in the knowledge that his need for her was so strong, he was losing his iron control. She would not disappoint him.

She made a circle with her thumb and forefinger, closing tightly around the base of his cock, and stroked all the way to the head. Garrett groaned, his eyes fluttering shut, and the bead of liquid at the tip of his cock grew larger.

She milked him again, then leaned forward to lick the bead from the head of his cock. His fingers buried themselves in her hair, pulling her closer as he thrust his cock into her mouth.

"Tease," he groaned.

"Is that an order?" she asked, as well as she could around a mouth full of cock.

"God, no!"

He slicked in and out of her mouth with short, urgent strokes while she loved him with her tongue and lips and teeth. Reaching up, she used one hand to squeeze and caress the length of his cock not in her mouth. Her other hand stroked and fondled his balls.

Garrett gasped and groaned, his breathy "Yes!" and "Oh God!" directing her to what pleased him most. He came in a fiery rush of fluid, filling her mouth and throat. Anne swallowed, then sucked his limp cock, draining it of the last of his seed.

He shuddered, stroking her hair, and slowly slipped his cock free of her wet mouth.

"Oh, God. I think you've killed me."

Anne just smiled, content to kneel at her master's feet. She'd see him every two weeks while he was away in London and Paris, and then they'd be together forever. Her body hummed with anticipation. Then her pesky logical brain interrupted.

"How did you arrange to see me every two weeks while you're away?"

"I made that one of the conditions in the deal for my promotion. Instead of a raise, I wanted two round-trip business class tickets each month between New York and London. Sometimes I'll come here, sometimes you can go there, but the point is, we'll be together."

Anne nuzzled her cheek against his damp cock, inhaling his beloved musky odor, and stroked his thighs in a soft caress that was half hug. "I don't care where I am, as long as I can be with you."

He pushed himself away from the wall and gently disentangled himself from her embrace. Bending over, he grabbed the pants that had fallen around his ankles, and quickly pulled them up. As he refastened the belt, he said, "Right now, where we need to be is at the restaurant."

"Oh! I'd forgotten about that." Anne sprang to her feet, tugging her clothing into order. She pulled her comb from her purse and whisked it through her hair, getting rid of the passionate furrows Garrett had plowed. A quick swipe of clear lip gloss restored the shine to her deep purple lip paint.

Garrett pulled a handkerchief from his pocket and wiped the telltale gloss from his own lips. "We're a little rumpled, but it's a dark restaurant. No one will notice."

He paused, his gaze raking over Anne. "There's a lot that no one would notice. And if you're a good, obedient slave, I'll do it all to you."

Her nipples tightened in anticipation, and she stroked a finger suggestively along the heavy gold of her collar. "I am yours, master. And I'm very, very good."

Epilogue

Two years later...

Anne smiled and nodded as she clicked her mouse on the last page of the presentation. "Great. You hit it the first time out. Those changes were just what I was looking for."

The young man on the opposite side of her desk let out the breath he'd been holding. She'd told Todd he wasn't leaving until the customer presentation was complete, even if it meant he'd be working the entire weekend, and her employees knew better than to question her when she gave them a deadline.

Anne glanced at her watch. It was just after six o'clock. "I'll send these off to Timpkin now, so he can review them over the weekend."

"So, you won't need me for anything else?"

She smiled at him, and made shooing motions. "Go. Enjoy your weekend. You earned it."

Todd hustled out the door of her office before she could change her mind and give him any other assignments. She heard the distant banging of drawers as he got ready to leave, then tuned out the noise and focused on composing the letter to her client.

She had her own reasons for wanting to quit work and get home. Garrett was visiting this weekend. Her fingertips brushed the agate bead dangling from her gold choker in a gesture that had long since become a habit.

His plane would arrive at 8:15. Maybe as early as eight, if the wind was right. Half an hour to get from the airport to her brownstone.

Her pulse quickened with anticipation. Even after two years, she only had to think about the man and her body turned to Jell-O. And in only one more month, he'd be coming home for good. She'd already blocked vacation days for the week of his return. She planned an enthusiastic celebration of his promotion to partner, and hoped he wouldn't let her out of the bed all week.

A muffled boom echoed through the deserted office. The double doors of heavy wood looked impressive, but they never closed properly unless you slammed them.

Reminded by the sound that she was still at her desk, she turned her attention once again to the client letter. Soon it was completed, and after giving it one last read through, she attached the presentation file and sent it off. She checked her task list for the final time, reassuring herself that all was in readiness for her meeting with Timpkin on Monday. Breathing out a sigh that sounded suspiciously like Todd's, she closed the Timpkin file and shut down her computer.

A distant rattle attracted her attention. Someone was shaking the doors in their frame. The building's security guard didn't check the office suites until after nine o'clock. Todd must have left something in his desk again. Last weekend, he'd forgotten the tickets to the concert he and his girlfriend were supposed to go to, and she'd followed him up to the office while he retrieved the tickets, lecturing him on his irresponsibility the entire time.

Chuckling, Anne stood up. "Hang on, Todd. I'll be right there."

As she opened the locked door, she asked, "What did you forget this time?"

"I forgot how hot you look in a business suit," Garrett answered.

"Garrett!" She threw her arms around his neck and kissed him, molding her lips to his. They broke the kiss to breathe, and she leaned back to look into his face. "I didn't expect you until 8:30."

"I caught the four o'clock flight instead of the six."

"The four? But the markets aren't closed by four."

He grinned, a devilish light sparking his dark eyes. "Trading was dead today, and my assistant was more than willing to cover for me when I explained it was a matter of *amore*."

Anne glanced downward, noting the obvious bulge in his slacks. "You keep your heart in your pants, do you?"

"Disrespectful wench. What's a master to do when his slave is so rude?"

She smiled and took a step backward. "I shall have to be shown the error of my ways."

Garrett followed her into the office suite, the door thumping closed behind him. "I plan on showing you a number of things. That's just one of them."

Anticipation skittered over the surface of Anne's skin like heat lightning. She swallowed, her mouth suddenly dry. "Whatever you say, master."

He turned her around and pointed her toward her office. She started walking, putting as much sway and swivel into her steps as she could. Garrett's sharp intake of breath made her smile, pleased with her obvious success.

"I do love to watch you walk when you're wearing a miniskirt," he murmured.

As she entered her office, he caught up with her, grabbing her from behind and pulling her against him so she could feel the strength of his erection. One arm held her pinned tightly in place, while his other hand roamed over her hips and thighs.

"Turn around," he whispered. "And on your knees."

She turned to face him, then knelt on the carpeting before him. He ripped open a condom packet, and handed her the rolled condom.

"Don't use your hands."

Anne licked her lips. When Garrett's hot gaze tracked the motion of her tongue, she did it again, in slow motion. He groaned.

With a short, savage jerk, he pulled open his belt, then unzipped his pants and let them drop to the floor. His cock sprung outward, eager to find its home in Anne's equally eager body.

She tipped her head back, unrolled the first half inch of the condom, and placed it in her mouth. Garrett grabbed her by the hair, mock savagery cloaking his careful positioning of her head so that she would not injure her neck. Then the head of his cock was pressing against her open lips, forcing her mouth wider. She resisted, knowing that opening her mouth would drop the condom, and he confidently forced his way past her resistance. Slowly, he entered her, his hot cock slipping between her wet lips, the condom unrolling and sheathing him as he pressed further and further into her mouth.

He entered her as fully as he could, the tip of his condom-covered cock sliding into her throat, and held the position for an eternity of exquisite torture before slipping himself out of her mouth. The condom glistened with wet saliva, a silent promise of other fluids that would anoint it momentarily.

"Stand up."

She did as he ordered, then removed her pantyhose and stepped backward when he ordered that, too. The back of her thighs hit the edge of her desk.

"Up on the desk."

Anne braced her hands on the edge of the desk and hopped up, so that she was sitting on the smooth surface. Garrett pushed her legs apart, shoving her miniskirt practically to her waist, and moved to stand between her thighs.

Starting at her knees, he trailed his fingertips over her skin in swirling patterns, gradually working his way up the sensitive skin of her inner thighs until he brushed the damp lace of her panties.

"Lace?" he asked. "Since when do you wear lace underpants to work?"

"I knew I'd be working late. I wasn't sure I'd have time to change when I got home."

His fingers brushed the swollen flesh behind the lace. She moaned, arching into his touch.

"So you've been thinking about me all day?" he asked, cupping his hand against the lace and rocking it against her. "Every time that lace stroked against your sex, you were imagining my touch?"

"Yes," she breathed.

He slipped a finger beneath the thin barrier of lace, and slid it inside her with a single, smooth motion. "I can tell. You're wet and ready. You want me."

"Yes, master."

Garrett rocked his hand against her again, one finger still deep inside her. Anne moaned, and bucked against the teasing pressure, wanting more.

"You need me, hot and hard and filling the space inside you."

"Yes, master." She writhed against his firm touch, aching for him to replace his finger with his cock.

He skimmed his thumb over the throbbing bud of her clitoris, and Anne gasped, convulsing beneath his skillful torture.

"Please, master. Please."

His thumb flicked back and forth over the swollen bud, wrenching a shaky moan from her throat with each touch, as her hips jumped and spasmed, instinctively trying to find and match the rhythm of his random caresses.

"Please," she begged. "Tell me what you want me to do. I'll do anything for you."

"Yes, I know you would. You're a good slave." His finger stroked a deep circle inside her, and his thumb pressed hard against her burning clitoris.

Anne sighed with pleasure, but all too soon he stopped the loving strokes, leaving her more aroused and aching than she had been. When he pulled his hand free, she had to bite her lip to keep from protesting.

Both his hands slid under her miniskirt and over her hips, grasping the waistband of her panties. Guessing his intent, she lifted her hips, and he pulled off the panties. They fell to the carpet, and Garrett kicked them aside.

"Do this for me then, my dear, sweet, slave. Show me how important I am to you by ignoring your own needs. Don't move. And don't come."

Anne caught her breath, her eyes locked to his burning gaze. "Yes, master. Anything for you."

He held her by the hips, tugging her forward slightly so that she was balanced on the very edge of her desk. Pinning her in place, he stepped forward, and rested the tip of his cock against her sensitive flesh. Anne gripped her desk with both hands, and did not tremble.

"Remember, don't move," he cautioned her again.

"Like a statue."

He pressed forward, sliding between her folds, slipping into position. Then his hands on her hips tightened, holding her down, and he thrust into her, sheathing his full length. Anne gasped, but remained still.

"A statue," Garrett said, his voice rough and slightly breathless. He pushed her away, leaning back so that his cock slid almost completely out, then surged forward while he pulled her toward him, maximizing the pounding impact of their union.

An involuntary whimper escaped Anne's throat. He repeated the action, changing his stance slightly each time so that his cock never stroked the same place twice. The hot, hard length of him seemed dipped in liquid fire, burning her wherever he stroked, but never returning to ease the flames of need he ignited. Soon she was vocalizing with his every thrust, mewling and whimpering in painful need.

Garrett fumbled with the buttons on her suit jacket, opening it and pulling it off of her. Her camisole followed a moment later. Then he lifted her breasts out of her bra, the elastic stretching tight beneath them. She imagined that she could already feel them swelling, growing more sensitive to his touch.

He pushed her backwards, sprawling her onto her desk. The Timpkin file fell from the desk, opening in mid-tumble to strew papers onto the carpeting like a shower of giant sized confetti. The pen carousel followed it down, a rainbow of pens rolling to the far corners of the office.

The change in angle increased the friction as he pumped into her, sending Anne perilously close to the edge. But she wouldn't disappoint him by coming too soon. She could hold on a little longer. Somehow.

As he thrust into her, even deeper than before, he bent over her and bit her swollen nipple.

Anne cried out as lightning flashed between her breast and his thrusting cock. Despite her best efforts, her hips and legs started to tremble.

He slid almost all the way out, then rammed his cock home and bit her other nipple.

"I can't do it," she moaned. "It's too much."

"Yes, you can." Garrett kissed both of her nipples, the sweet encouragement nearly undoing her. Then he pulled her hips tight against his, fully sheathing his cock inside her, and pressed her thighs to his waist. "Lock your legs behind me."

He lifted her up so that she straddled him, riding his cock, and pressed her back against the wall. His hips swiveled, rolling his cock inside her, faster and faster, while he whispered to her how beautiful, brilliant, and desirable she was. Tears streamed down her face unchecked as she gasped and panted, barely able to make sense of his words. But her heart floated and soared in the same euphoric daze as her body.

"I love you, Anne," he whispered. "I want to love every inch of you."

He leaned into her, holding her against the wall with his weight, and freeing his hands to explore. They slid up under her miniskirt, cupping and caressing her ass. He toyed with her opening, teasing the sensitive nerves by circling his finger around and around the edge until she was growling and whining, begging for relief with sound and inflection, incapable of finding and using words.

Garrett pressed the fingers of one hand into her opening, and she cried out, almost overcome by the pleasure. His fingers moved, reaching inside her, and trapping her pulsing flesh between his questing fingers and thrusting cock.

She drew a deep breath to scream, but never got the chance because he chose that moment to kiss her. His mouth devoured hers, bruising her lips with his passion, then sucking and biting the swollen skin. He forced her mouth open, and plunged his tongue inside. Capturing her tongue and pulling it into his own mouth, he sucked her in time with his thrusting fingers and cock.

Anne trembled, balanced on the taut edge of release.

Gasping, he pulled his mouth away.

"Now," he said. "Now you may come."

His hands and cock increased the speed of their thrusting, banging Anne against the wall. She tightened her grip around his waist and wrapped her arms around his neck, riding him as hard as he could go. Garrett's breath rasped in ragged gasps as he pushed harder, faster.

Anne felt the final spiral take hold, and clutched him convulsively. He pumped and thrust, taking her higher and higher, until she reached the peak and leapt into soaring flight. A moment later, he tensed, thrust deeply, and held himself there, trembling, until he too found his release.

She awoke, lying on the carpet, deliciously sore and perfectly content. Garrett was kneeling in front of the pen carousel, biting his lip in concentration as he attempted to figure out the order and rationale she had used to organize her pens.

Anne giggled. "Don't bother. They're in order by Pantone number. You'll never figure it out."

He turned and smiled down at her. Anne felt her heart blossoming beneath the radiance of his smile.

"Dear, sweet, Anne. I said it while we were making love, but I want to say it again when you can understand me. I love you."

"Garrett..." Words failed her. She'd long since stopped waiting to hear the magical phrase, trusting the love she saw in his actions, and resigning herself to the fact that he was one of those men who just couldn't say the words. Now it was she who couldn't express how she felt. Hopefully her teary eyes and trembling smile made her point.

A lightning fast grin flickered across his face. "I've reduced you to being unable to speak again, and I didn't even need sex to do it."

"Garrett, I—"

"Shh." He placed his finger against her lips, silencing her. "Two years ago today I gave you my collar. Now I have another piece of jewelry for you, if you will consent to wear it."

He reached into the inside pocket of his jacket, and pulled out a much smaller jeweler's box. Cracking the lid, he revealed the brilliant white fire of a diamond solitaire.

"Anne Logan, beloved, will you do me the honor of agreeing to be my wife?"

This time, she had no trouble finding the word. "Yes."

Garrett slid the ring onto her finger, then leaned down to give her a kiss of the same dazzling brilliance as the diamond. Some time later, Anne blinked owlishly, and found herself sitting in his lap on the floor, nestled in his arms.

"Mm, this is nice," he said, nuzzling the side of her neck.

She lifted her hand to admire her engagement ring, turning it back and forth to catch the light. A stray beam of light glanced off the face of her watch, and she froze in surprise. How did it get to be 8:45 already?

Garrett continued nuzzling her neck, expanding his investigation to the intriguing plane of her shoulder. "I'd like to just stay with you here forever."

"I'd like nothing better than to stay by your side for the rest of my life. But not here."

The urgency in her tone broke through to him, and he lifted his head from his nuzzling. "Why not?"

"Because in fifteen minutes the security guard will be making his rounds. And we didn't lock the door."

Garrett's eyes widened, then he began to laugh. "So much for the myth of marriage making a man more respectable."

His laughter faded, and he smiled tenderly at her before setting Anne on her feet, and handing her a pile of her discarded clothing. "Let's go home."

POWER PLAY

Written by

MADELEINE OH

Chapter One

"There you are!" Claudine spread soothing oil on Annie's newly-waxed pussy, her fingers felt cool against the sensitized flesh. "Looks beautiful, if I say so myself. All set for your birthday Saturday night?"

Was she? It had seemed a brilliant idea at the time. "I think so." Too wishy-washy, this was a one-time professional dominatrix she was talking to. "Yes, I'm ready. Is Tom?"

Claudine let out a deep throaty chuckle. "Don't worry, Annie. Tom will be ready when I tell him." Annie didn't doubt it. Seeing how Tom Baldwin, the heartthrob of half the female viewing population, followed his mistress's wishes, had been as much an education as Annie's own tutelage in submission from her lover, Mark. Claudine eyed her handiwork critically. "How is it feeling?"

"Easing off." Now the hurt was fading, the slow tingle she remembered from last time built with each sweep of Claudine's fingers. Before, Claudine eased everything by giving Annie a climax, but now...

"Good!" Claudine stepped back. "Sorry, Annie," she said, as Annie sighed with disappointment. "Mark was most specific. No helping you out this time." Why was she not surprised? He, no doubt, wanted her panting for it by the time he got home.

When Claudine left the small room, Annie dressed, deliberately leaving off her panties and stuffing them in her handbag. Not purely out of deference to Mark's rules–she was still on her way home from work after all–but because the constant caress of the soft, well-washed cotton against her newly-denuded, and ultra-sensitive pussy, would drive her batty.

"See you Saturday," Claudine said, as Annie emerged, dressed, and hoping she looked far more composed than she felt. "Tom will be ready for you, I promise."

Annie only hoped she would be.

Try as she might, as she drove home through the early evening, Annie couldn't get her mind off the warm glow in her nether regions. Aching for it was the literal truth! If Mark hadn't specifically prohibited it, she'd be grabbing her trusty her vibrator the minute she got home.

As it was…

She stopped at the Fish and Chip shop in the village and bought a portion of doner kebab. She was back in the car and turning into the lane leading to her cottage, before the oddness of that hit her. The village chippie had changed–and so had she. She might still be called 'Cast-Iron Cavendish' behind her back by the children at school, but her journey into submission with Mark had been as unexpected, as it was thrilling. The headmaster, who only yesterday complimented her on her classroom discipline and her fellow teachers, who admired her knack of dealing with recalcitrant students, would never dream that at a word or nod from her lover, she would strip naked and kneel at this feet, offering herself for their mutual pleasure.

Just thinking about that was a rotten idea. Her pussy throbbed with an anticipation that was not going to get assuaged any time soon. Maybe a cold shower would work. It supposedly did for adolescents with raging hormones.

The cold shower left her shivering with goosebumps over every centimeter of her body. Annie turned on the hot water full blast until the bathroom steamed up, adjusted the temperature to bearable, and stood under the warming spray. For good measure she washed her hair, dried herself and her damp hair, and pulled on well-worn and washed-soft sweats and sheepskin slippers. If she didn't look sexy or alluring, maybe she wouldn't feel so randy.

She poured a glass of wine. Deciding to indulge herself she laid a place in her tiny dining room, using her grandmother's silver and one of the three antique Wedgwood plates she'd found in a market stall a few months back. Mehemet's doner kebab wasn't exactly fillet steak but after a long day at school, and a session with Claudine and hot wax, it was as welcome as a feast.

She'd taken three mouthfuls and two tastes of wine, when the phone rang.

It was Mark.

"Can't talk now, love," he said, his voice clear, despite the buzz of traffic in the background, "I'm in a taxi. Meeting just finished. Be at your computer at eight your time."

"Alright."

"Be ready!"

He broke the connection. She still had almost an hour. Plenty of time for a leisurely dinner and a second glass of wine, if she fancied it. But what she really fancied was Mark. Just imagining Mark's deep blue eyes gazing at her as she stood naked before him, sent her pussy purring.

Yeah! And right now she'd better finish dinner, clean up, grade the papers she'd brought home, and get finished by eight.

At least she didn't have to dress up. She knew, without Mark telling her, he expected her to be naked.

"Annie, are you naked?" Mark's question appeared in the screen in a string of flickering letters.

She pictured his fingers depressing each key just seconds before the letter appeared in her screen. "Yes, Mark."

"Wearing your collar?"

"Yes." Just! She'd almost forgotten and had zipped back to her dressing table to fasten it on while she watched the screen for his first message to appear.

"Good! If you'd forgotten, I'd have to punish you when I return, and I'd much rather fuck you."

She wouldn't argue with that. "When will you be back? I was at Claudine's spa this afternoon and she asked. I told her Friday."

"So you went."

"Of course. You asked me to."

"You do everything I ask, don't you Annie?"

Her throat tightened at that. Good thing she didn't have to speak. "Yes, Mark."

"You keep your lovely pussy waxed, just to please me, don't you?"

"Yes, but it pleases me too." Had she really typed that? Yes! And meant it.

"How, Annie?"

She hesitated as her body quickened. "I like the way my knickers rub my bare flesh, and…"

"You wore knickers, Annie? What about my rules?"

"Not after I left the spa, Mark. But I will tomorrow, when I go to school, and they will feel like a slow caress against my bare pussy. It keeps thinking of you."

An emoticon :-) appeared on the screen. "Anything else it does to you? "

"Reminds me I'm yours." Her chest tightened, as she read words she barely remembered typing.

"Yes, you are, aren't you, my love? Now's your chance to show me, and if you please me, you'll get rewarded."

What now? The screen stayed blank several moments. Of course! It was her turn to reply. "I'll do my best."

"I know. On your knees!"

How in the name of sanity was this going to work? On her knees, her keyboard was at eye level. Her touch typing wasn't that good! She reached up and pulled the keyboard down on the carpet in front of her. That worked fine, but she'd give herself whiplash between the screen on her desk and the keyboard on the floor. There had to be a better way... "Just a moment, please, Mark."

"What's the matter?"

"Keyboard complications!" What now? She had it! Annie put her keyboard on the seat of her desk chair. She could comfortably type and watch the monitor at the same time. "I've got it now."

"You'll be getting it in a while, if you please me, Annie. Are your thighs open?"

Dear heaven, Mark! Were they? Annie spread her knees wider. She could only manage so far before her thigh muscles protested. "As wide as I can get them."

"Good, my love. Now, slowly, as nothing tonight is to be hurried, caress your left nipple." Three gentle circles with her finger and the nipple was hard and ready, and her heartbeat racing. Annie shut her eyes, imagining it was Mark's touch not her own. "Is it hard yet?"

"Yes."

"Good. Open the bottom left drawer of your desk."

Where she kept spare paper for the printer? Why? Annie nudged along on her knees and pulled the drawer open. Her purple suede pussy whip--the flogger Mark gave her soon after they met--sat on the topmost pack of heavyweight super white. She shivered, remembering the kiss of the slim thongs on her flesh. Did Mark expect her to whip herself? Surely not? Why not? Could she? Could she not? She was already wet between her legs, just looking at the narrow curled tails of soft suede that either stung or caressed depending on the force behind Mark's arm. Remembering Mark, Annie glanced up at her monitor.

"ANNIE?"

"Yes?"

"You obeyed, I hope. What did you find?"

"Our pussy whip." Her heart thudded. The whip was 'theirs' — his to wield, and hers to receive.

"You're distracted, Annie. Concentrate. What else is there?"

Four packs of paper was the wrong answer. She brushed aside the suede thongs, to find nipple clamps, her mouth going dry as she stared at the shiny metal. "Nipple cramps" she typed, barely taking her eyes off them.

"Pay attention, Annie!" Mark replied. "But I'm sure they will cramp! Take one, make sure your left nipple is as hard as you can make it, and clamp it."

It wasn't the putting on, it was the rush of sensation when they came off, she hated, and Mark knew it. Annie frowned at the clamp in the palm of her hand, and closed her damp fist. Her nipple didn't need any more hardening, but she took the time to warm the clamp, to make the going on easier. The pinch of the metal she felt deep in her pussy. As the sharp sting in her nipple eased to an achy numbness, she took a deep breath and exhaled slowly. "It's on, Mark."

"Wonderful, Annie. If I parted your lovely cunt lips, I'd see you damp and ready. Wouldn't I?"

"Yes."

"Good. I'll reward you for that...later. Now, what do you think I'll ask next?"

"To put on the other clamp?" Hell, why did she suggest it? One was more than enough.

"Not yet! But I'm happy to see you so eager. Just one for now. I want you to savor the different sensations in your nipples. How does the left feel?"

"Aching and burning, it's not fully numb yet."

"Good! How about the other one?"

"It's tingling too." Didn't make sense but it was: a slow, not unpleasant, throb.

"And your pussy?"

"Wet." Her fingers trembled as she typed. She was ready, and Mark would make her wait.

"Wonderful! I love you, Annie. Remember your safe word?"

"Yes, Annette Sophia Cavendish."

"How was school today?"

"Alright. No panics. No unsanctioned fire drills, like last week. But I did get volunteered to do the Christmas Play."

"LOL! What are you doing?"

"The head wanted Amahl and the Night Visitors, but since Bill Waite, who used to do the music has gone, I said that was beyond me. So we're doing the Christmas Carol, lots of extra parts, so we can have umpteen kids in it."

"Squeeze your other nipple as hard as you can." How like Mark to switch from Scrooge and Ghosts of Christmas to nipple torture! But with only the slightest hesitation, Annie pinched her right nipple between thumb and index finger. "Pull your nipple out," Mark typed. Annie stretched the sensitive flesh. "Now put on the other clamp." She gritted her teeth as the felt-padded teeth closed down.

The ache was at least even now, but her pussy was positively tingling.

What next? Annie took a couple deep breaths, exhaled slowly, and typed, "What should I do now, Mark."

There were no other clips, and no clothes pegs either, but the soft tresses of her flogger almost sang to her. She wanted their caress, and the slow, warm sting that followed. She needed to feel the bite on her skin, and the moist response between her legs. She ached for the wild climax that would follow, when Mark ordered her to come. And she was stuck on her knees, alone, with Mark on the other side of the English Channel.

"Annie?"

"Yes."

"Pick up the whip..." Annie reached out-- turning her shoulders slowly so as not to jiggle her breasts and set the clamps pulling--and closed her hand over the smooth, suede-covered handle. She swiveled back equally carefully, and saw the end of Mark's order, "...and do exactly what I tell you."

"Yes, Mark."

"You are forbidden to come until I give the word."

Quite literally! Resisting the temptation to ask what he wanted, Annie waited, the whip loose in her hand, the tresses hanging slack by her thighs, and her nipples numb from the clips. Her breath came smooth and even but her heart raced with anticipation.

"Are you holding the whip in your right hand?"

"Yes."

"Trail it down your left arm. Slowly." Soft as a caress she stroked her skin with the suede thongs, raising goosebumps, and heightening awareness of her body and her needs. "Now the right arm." She switched hands, and obeyed. "Down between your breasts to just below your navel. No lower!" It was hard to stop. A couple more inches and the soft tresses would tease the top of her slit. Mark would never know...but she would. She stopped, brushing the ends against her belly. "Repeat that. Twice."

Not hard to obey. Except her breath was catching and her heart beating faster than ever. "Stroke the front of your thighs...the backs." Harder, but no hardship. Her skin tingled with the touch of suede on flesh, and her cunt flowed with anticipation. Mark didn't let her down. "Back and forth between your legs."

Little moans accompanied the soft tails catching her sensitized flesh. She slowed her hand, as the wild spirals of arousal heightened and rushed her mind.

Whip still in hand, she typed. "I'm conning!"

"Not until you learn to spell, Annie!"

Groaning, Annie dropped the darn whip on the carpet, and typed, "I'm coming!"

"Yes, love. I'm not surprised. I know how that arouses you. But not until I give you permission."

A slow, agonized sound rose from deep in her belly. But she waited. Mark's orders came slow and certain. More caresses with suede. Four slaps on her back, two over each shoulder, stinging but arousing her all the more. "Now. Slow as you know how, down across your breasts...your belly, tease your cunt just a little more. Stop! Count to seven and resume."

His orders continued: words chasing phrases across the screen. The pace quickened. Annie panted, a soft sheen of sweat gathering on her naked body. A stroke across her breast caught one clamp, eliciting a yelp, but on she followed, Mark's directions increasing her need, and peaking her arousal. Sighs accompanied each touch of the whip. Annie whimpered, flicking the soft tresses against her now open, and ready, pussy. How much longer?

"Nearly ready, Annie?"

"Yes." It took all her concentration to type three letters.

"Good. Yank off those clamps."

Biting her lip, she braced for the sting of returning circulation. "Up your thighs with the whip, down, and back, again, again." She obeyed, panting, sighing and sweating until the long awaited words appeared. "Come, Annie! Come for me!"

Before the last word appeared, her mind leapt: soaring to ecstasy as, with a great ripple of pleasure, her body convulsed, her knees gave way, and she ended up a tangled, sweaty heap on the carpet.

"Alright, Annie?"

How long those last two words sat on the screen, she had no idea. Could have been an hour while her body climaxed and her mind raced. "Yes, Mark," she typed with shaking hands. "I love you."

"Mutual, my love," he typed. "Now go to bed."

Holding onto the chair, she managed to stand, but barely remembered to shut down her computer, before curling up under her duvet. She was alone, but not lonely. Her body still thrummed with the joy of Mark's power, and the thrill of a bone-weakening climax.

She had no trouble sleeping.

Chapter Two

"Doing anything special for your birthday, Annie?"

Annie smiled at Jim, the new History teacher, who'd insisted a crowd of them stop off at a local pub and buy Annie a drink to celebrate. She also suspected he was angling for a chance to ask her out.

She took a sip of her gin and tonic. "I'm spending the weekend with some friends in London."

"Give up, Jim," Sally-who-taught-Art said, "Annie's heart is taken. "

"Drat!" He sounded half-downcast, half-joking. "I planned a weekend of passion, Annie. I'd have wined and dined you."

"Mark's going to do that." And maybe tie her up, and whip her, to say nothing of what she'd be doing with Tom. Jim couldn't compete.

"By the look on your face, you're hoping for more than wining and dining." Sally grinned.

"Maybe, but I've no intention of sharing!"

"Pooh!" Sally tipped her glass and drank. "You'd better tell all on Monday."

When pigs did needlepoint!

As she drove home, Annie's mind swung between the bantering of her colleagues--who'd no doubt have strokes if they knew an nth part of it-- and the reality of Mark. But, where once she'd felt torn, even split in two by the opposing tugs of her life, now she longed for Mark and the erotic torture at his hands. Heck, she didn't even need his hands! She'd climaxed at seeing his command as a line of text on the screen. Just thinking about it made her knickers damp. Mark's rule of not wearing them made sense, but she'd be home soon and have them off. He'd call her when he got in, and tomorrow they'd be together, until the time came for Tom.

She wriggled against the seat at that thought. She liked Tom. Incredible as it seemed, he was a pal, but that didn't stop her from indulging in the fantasies shared by half the female viewing population. But in two short weeks the past summer, she'd learned far more about Tom Baldwin than his legions of swooning admirers could ever imagine. She'd also come face to face with her own sexual needs. At the time she'd been confused and torn, but now she'd happily come to terms with her own submissive needs and Mark was only too happy to satisfy them. Heck, he'd recognized them before she knew they existed.

At the thought of her lover, she grinned, a man who could give her a mind-shattering climax over cyberspace, was a man to keep.

It was only after she got home and curled up with a book for the evening, that doubts attacked her: What in the name of sanity was she going to do tomorrow?

In a fit of pique and, she had to admit, a smidgen of illicit fascination, she'd asked for Tom for her birthday, expecting to get a rise out of Mark, and maybe shock him. Instead, she received what she asked for...almost. Mark and Claudine's only stipulation was that they orchestrate the scene. Hardly surprising really, she could hardly expect two dominants to hand over all the controls. But what was she going to do? Follow the script they wrote for her, of course. She'd just like to get to read it before tomorrow. But...wasn't 'trust' Mark's watchword? She'd trusted him so far, she would over this. She relished the thought of once again laying into Tom's broad shoulders and firm butt, and the thought of an undisturbed fuck wasn't half bad.

She still wondered at Mark's ready acquiescence, but he'd handed her over to John, and seemed the least jealous of any man she'd ever know. Non-jealous but utterly possessive, and how she enjoyed being owned.

They chose a definitely unfashionable restaurant—for good reason. The last thing Tom Baldwin wanted was gossip columnists speculating on his dinner companions. The ambiance was cramped and noisy, but the food in the little restaurant was marvelous. Or rather the aromas of spices, garlic, cheese, and baking were marvelous. Annie ate virtually nothing. Her antipasti went back almost untouched, prompting the waiter to inquire if everything was all right, and now she toyed with her veal.

"Eat up, Annie!" Tom said with a grin. "You'll need your strength!"

That, she didn't doubt. But she wasn't likely to get it from Saltimbocca ala Romagna.

She'd managed a couple of bites, had even tasted them, when Claudine said, "Mark, you've got to tell her. Annie's too worried to eat."

Mark paused, as if to consider the option, but shook his head. "No, we agreed to share the particulars over dessert. Annie can wait that long." He did, however, reach over and squeeze her hand. "Trust me Annie, what we have orchestrated, you can do." His 'trust me' worked, almost like a magic charm. If he had confidence, why did she doubt herself?

"It's Tom we're wondering about," Claudine said, a smile twitching the corner of her mouth. She looked sideways at her submissive. "What about it , Tom?"

"You know I can, Boss. Or you wouldn't allow me."

Claudine nodded. "Don't disappoint Annie, Tom. She's got her hopes up!"

Given Tom's long years of experience, Annie momentarily wondered about Claudine's doubts. Seemed more likely she'd be the one disappointing. Heck she still didn't know what scene Mark and Claudine had planned, but a smile from Mark reassured Annie utterly. She could control a classroom of wiggly ten-year-old boys, and even in an earlier job, a couple of dozen hormone-crazed teenagers, she could surely control one, solitary sex-symbol. She took another bite of veal and speared an asparagus tip.

"Looks a bit phallic doesn't it, Annie?" Tom asked with a grin.

She gave him her best 'witchy teacher' look and he grinned wider. This was not going to be the same. But his smile and the wicked light in his eyes did restore her appetite.

She took care of the veal and her tiramisu, but almost snorted her espresso across the table onto Claudine when Mark said, "Annie, I'm counting on your utter submission to Tom."

She gratefully took the napkin Mark handed her. After wiping her mouth and nose, she looked over the edge of the crisp line and up at her lover. "That wasn't what I asked for!"

"You asked for Tom for a night." Smug was not the word for the look on his face.

"I meant to dominate him. I thought you knew that!"

"Yes," he agreed, "but you'll do far better as a submissive. Claudine and I talked this over--at length as it happens--and decided this suited you much better. "

The fact she'd had the same thought didn't help. "Mark, you knew exactly what I wanted!"

"Yes, love. But this is what I've planned. You don't have to agree, you know that. But if you do go with Tom, he tops."

Annie took a deep breath, carefully not looking in Tom's direction. "I think I need another espresso." She really needed a very stiff drink, but needed a clear head even more.

"Will that really help you decide?" Claudine asked.

"No, but it will buy me a little time while I panic quietly."

"Why panic?" Tom asked. He spoke so quietly that she instinctively leaned forward to hear him. "I know your limits. Mark and Claudine just about beat them into me!"

Annie's mouth went dry at the thought of Tom, naked, his tanned skin glistening with sweat, strong arms stretched over his head as he hung from the ceiling, and Mark and Claudine alternately hitting him as they grilled him. She swallowed. Slowly. "When did they beat you?"

"Alternate evenings for the last two weeks. It was a relief when Mark went off to Brussels. Gave me a bit of a break, or would have if Claudine hadn't made up for it. She and Mark have it all laid out." Her reached across and took her hand. "Trust me, Annie. I memorized every limit on your list. I won't give you more than you want. But I promise not to disappoint you."

She needed a week to go home and consider this new twist. She didn't even have fifteen minutes.

Options? Clear as the sparkling water she'd sipped throughout dinner. Two choices: to go with Tom or not. She was free to refuse, and forever wonder what she'd missed. "You promise you won't disappoint?"

Tom raised three fingers to the dark curl that hung over his forehead. "Scout's honor!"

"Were you really a Boy Scout?"

"Hell, yes! I'll have you know I was a patrol leader: the Wolf patrol. "

She didn't even try to hold back the chuckle at the image of Tom in khaki shorts and lanyard. "Aptly named!"

"Yes! I plan to eat you alive."

"This has rather changed my plans. I have my lovely suede whip in Mark's car."

"It's in my car now." His fingers meshed with hers and squeezed gently. "Coming?"

Annie stood up, and remembered Mark and Claudine were still sipping espresso and Strega. Or had been before Mark got up and smiled. "I'll see you to the door. I want to make sure you get safely away."

Annie walked through the restaurant in a fog. It was really happening! She glanced sideways at Mark and he smiled, his blue eyes dancing with the same light that glimmered when he had her trussed and bound. He was enjoying this. Her agreement pleased him. More than pleased! He looked delighted. His giving her to Tom, underscored his ownership. Her heart thudded inside her ribs. "Mark," she whispered as Tom held the door for them to step out onto the street.

Mark kissed her gently, silencing her unspoken question. "Do you want to safeword out?"

"I just wanted to ask when…"

He shook his head. "No, Annie–unless you want to refuse this. You're Tom's, until I reclaim you. Any questions you ask of him." Mark raised her hand and turning it palm up, kissed the soft tender skin before curling her fingers into a closed fist and placing her hand in Tom's. "She's precious and wonderful Tom. Take care of her. Use her well."

Tom's hand closed tightly, grasping her fist in his. "She'll come back to you safe and sound, Mark, but maybe with a few marks on her."

Annie shivered. She opened her mouth to ask what he was marking her with, but Tom pressed her lips closed with his finger. "Hush, Annie! Not a word! Speak when I ask a direct question, otherwise you may only open your lips to take in my cock, or use your safeword."

Anne stared at Mark. He'd never made that rule! She expected him to contradict Tom, but instead he smiled and dropped a soft kiss on her head. "Make me proud."

She felt downright giddy as Tom unlocked the passenger door, and held it open. Her knees wobbled and goosebumps peppered her skin. Mark kissed her: a slow, possessive branding, as his lips opened her mouth and pressed hard and his tongue touched hers. Annie moaned as he pulled her against him and his obvious erection. His hands ruffled her hair as he held her head steady and kissed deeper. She leaned into him, absorbing his scent, his power, and his taste, as her body and mind responded to his embrace. He eased his lips off hers. "Obey Tom, as you would me," he whispered into her mouth, and before she could even think not to reply, Mark had her in the passenger seat, seat belt tight across her chest, and closed the door.

As she turned to wave goodbye, Tom revved the engine and pulled away from the curb. The curve of the street immediately hid her lover from view.

Chapter Three

She was alone in the dark, with her fantasy, and speeding off to who-knew-where, and as for what awaited when they arrived...

"Are those thigh highs?" Tom asked. "Take them off."

"Yes, they are, and I..."

"Annie, I need obedience, not conversation. Get them off!"

Definitely not the easy-going, submissive Tom! Annie rolled down the fine nylon and had her mouth open to ask what he wanted her to do with them, when she remembered, and waited. He smiled, as if sensing her almost-question, and held out his hand. "I'll take them. They'll come in handy if I need to tie you up."

Whether it was the promise in his words, or the touch of his hand, she'd never know, but her body went into overdrive: wetness gathered between the legs, her heart raced, and her skin tingled at the prospect of Tom binding her wrists and ankles with her cast-off stockings.

How much longer until they reached his flat? Tom lived somewhere in the docklands, Mark had told her. She wanted to ask but bit her lip. If Tom thought she couldn't keep quiet, he was in for a surprise.

"Annie, open the glove compartment, please," Tom said after several minutes, "and take out the blindfold."

How like Mark to be sure Tom had a blindfold! He'd no doubt told him it scared her...and aroused her like nobody's business. Among the notepads, a box of condoms, and a pair of cashmere-lined gloves, Annie found the blindfold: soft black leather lined with black silk. As she pulled it out, and the ribbons on either end brushed her skin, one tail wrapping around her wrist.

Tom said, "Hold on to it. You'll put it on, in a minute."

Taking a deep breath, Annie leaned back against the leather upholstery and closed her eyes, imagining the brush of silk against her eyelids, the sense of isolation in darkness, and the thrill of the wait for the first kiss of suede, or the sharp sting of a male hand, and the sweet warmth under her skin. Fingers tightening on the leather in her lap, Annie wondered about their destination. They were beyond Putney on the A3. Going away from London. But where?

"My weekend cottage."

Annie almost jumped, and turned to Tom, waiting for more explanation. It wasn't forthcoming. After Mark's habit of eliciting conversation, and encouraging her to talk about everything from difficult parents and her plans for redecorating her kitchen, to her preferred shape of butt plugs, Tom's silence was a strain. Which was no doubt the whole idea.

She'd know exactly where they were going when they got there...until then...Annie shut her eyes and thought about Tom's wonderfully broad cock, and how it would feel, sliding deep into her. The swift, clandestine fuck in the pantry that morning in Cornwall had been far too brief--and too soon interrupted--to fully appreciate Tom Baldwin's male assets. But soon...

"Annie, put on the blindfold." Her fingers trembled but she managed. "Make sure it's snug. Lean back. Get comfortable." The smell of soft leather filled the dark. "Spread your legs. " Her skirt rode up. She tried to smooth it down, but stopped as Tom closed his hand over her wrist. "Ease your skirt up to expose your thighs. Open them wider."

She hoped Tom stayed under the speed limit. If they got stopped for speeding...

They didn't. The car purred south and Annie waited.

The sounds of bluegrass music filled the car. Tom sang along. He had a beautiful voice, with just the right twang. Had he once played blue grass? Hell if she knew! She knew precious little about him really, other than his sexual tastes. She was blindfolded, driving heaven knew where, with a man she barely knew!

She fought off the panic. Mark trusted Tom. So would she.

"Relax, Annie," Tom said, as if reading her mind. As he spoke, her seat eased back. Leaning backwards, legs wide, she was exposed and open, but oddly relaxed. Safe in the leather-lined cocoon of Tom's car, she shut her eyes behind the blindfold, and let her body relax to the sound of Lester Flatt and Earl Scruggs, and the scent of Tom's Eau Sauvage cologne. Might as well rest while she could. She'd seen enough at parties to know that Tom played hard.

"How do you touch yourself when you masturbate, Annie?"

"What?" she asked, as she came alert enough to process the question. She'd been half-dozing in the dark and quiet.

"You heard, Annie. How do you masturbate? "

She turned towards his voice. Imagining a little smile in the corners of his mouth as the blush rose up from her chin. Thank heavens for the dark! "I don't."

"Never?"

"Not since I've known Mark. I agreed not to. I come when he tells me to." Incredible, but oh, so true. And Mark always made it worth the wait.

"I see," Tom said. Annie hoped it was too dark for him to mean that literally. She was smirking at the memories of her last wild climax. "When was the last time he permitted you to climax? "

"Wednesday."

"This week? He was in Belgium."

"Yes. We instant messaged."

"A cyber climax! Time for some real life sex and submission. Unbutton your shirt and expose your breasts."

She hoped to heaven they were still on the main road. But knew in her heart knew Tom would never ask this while they drove through built up areas. The five pearl buttons were smooth and round. Finding them in the dark wasn't easy against the satin of her shirt. When she touched them, they slipped out of her fingers. It took forever to undo them all, but she managed, pushing her shirt open so her breasts hung free.

Tom's hand cupped her right breast. He squeezed her nipple. "Hard already! Hot for it aren't you Annie?" He tightened his hold. "Aren't you?" he repeated twisting enough to make her start, but not quite enough to hurt. He wanted an answer. But what? It was an 'any answer is the wrong answer ' question. Something Mark delighted in.

"I'm ready to follow your wishes."

"Whatever I ask?"

Her heart slowed for several beats before racing. "Yes," she replied, dry-mouthed. She smiled. Her mouth might have gone dry, but other parts definitely hadn't. Could Tom smell her arousal? How could he not? Her scent filled the car.

If it did, he ignored it. He gave her nipple a last, sharp squeeze as if for luck, and drove on in silence for several minutes.

"I play differently from Mark," Tom said at last.

What was she to make of that? Worry! That was most likely the whole point, and it worked--sort of. She was dying to ask, how? So she took another slow breath.

Behind the blindfold she was lost, isolated, unable to read the signposts, with no way to know how fast Tom drove, or how far they'd come. How long had it been? Ten minutes? Twenty? Could have been an hour. She'd drive herself batty if she went on this way. She let her mind slip. Might was well rest while she could. Once they arrived…

After a while, the car slowed. They veered to the left and went uphill, stopped and turned left. They had to be driving along a country lane. They slowed considerably and were no longer driving straight but turning bends and going round sharp corners. They came to a standstill, turned again and crawled over a bumpy road before stopping.

"Stay there while I unlock and take everything in," Tom said. Cool evening air followed as he opened the door. "I'll come back and get you in a jiffy."

It was a pretty long jiffy before he opened her door, unlatched her seat belt, and helped her to her feet. Taking off the darn blindfold would have made it a whole lot easier, but…

Tom undid it when they got inside. Annie blinked as she looked around. The lights were dim, thoughtful of him, bright lights would have half-blinded her. She stood in a wide room, with an inglenook fireplace, and chintz-covered furniture. Dark red velvet curtains hung at the windows. At one end of the room, a wide, open-tread staircase led to the floor above. At the other end, an open doorway gave onto the kitchen.

Annie looked all around and back again. She'd expected play equipment: a whipping horse perhaps, or the St Andrew's cross Mark's friends, Emma and Alistair brought out for parties…but instead she was standing in a nice, comfortable-looking country cottage.

Maybe Tom had a basement, or an equipped playroom upstairs, that neighbors and non-members of their special circle never saw.

"Like it?" Tom asked as he crossed the room and set a match to the fire.

Seemed more like her great-aunt's house in Rye than the country pad of a closet-kinky actor. "It's lovely."

"It's my secret hidey-hole. The press will never know about it. It's in my married half-sister's name, and I only come here by myself––or with Claudine."

And her. It was enough to give any woman pause. "Have you had it long?" Drat! "Sorry. Broke the rules again."

"Don't worry, at least not for now. We need to chat a bit. I did that in the car to make sure you could respond to me." He grinned. "You responded alright." And still was responding come to that! "Have a seat, look around if you like, and I'll make us some tea."

He had surprising her down to a fine art, but as dry as her mouth was, she was not about to turn down a cup of tea.

While Tom filled the kettle and clinked cups and saucers in the kitchen, Annie wandered over to his bookshelves. Tom read detective stories, science fiction, and kink erotica. Among his collection were most of the titles she'd slowly accumulated over the past few months. He must have loved "Just William", "Stig of the Dump", and "Narnia" as a boy. He still had the battered volumes, some complete with tattered dust covers.

"Here you are: milk, no sugar, right?"

She took the offered mug. "Thanks."

"Have a seat."

The matching chairs on either side of the fire were too much like her own twin chairs where she sat at Mark's feet. She took the sofa. Tom settled on the other end, his elbow resting on the wide arm, his feet propped on the coffee table. They both watched the fire for several seconds. Annie sipped her tea. It was still too hot to drink. "You wanted to talk."

"Right!" Tom nodded. "First, thanks for asking for me for your birthday." He grinned. "Gave my ego no end of a boost."

It was on the tip of her tongue to deny it, but why doubt his sincerity? He might be a national heartthrob, but how many of his adoring fans would be willing to let him tie them up and do who knew what? "We should both thank Mark and Claudine for agreeing."

He shook his head and took a sip of tea. "Listen, Annie, sub to sub talk here, okay? They are both getting a great big charge out of this." Her surprise had to show on her face. He shook his head. "You don't get it, do you? It's like this: Mark hands you to me. That proves he owns you. Gives his dominant soul no end of a boost. They both had the fun of teaching me your limits. Heck! Claudine strung me up and made me memorize them. Every time I slowed or hesitated she laid one into me. I tell you, it was damn hard to concentrate. Not only that, for the next six months she'll flay my arse while reminding me I'm on the receiving end, the way it should be!"

She didn't ask why he let Claudine do it to him. It would mean asking why she accepted Mark's domination, or why in a few minutes she'd take whatever Tom dished out. She'd given up questioning and accepted, it was her nature, and it felt right. And now... "But tonight they appointed you dominant."

"Top," he corrected her. "You'll be my bottom, not my sub. Subtle but major difference. We're just playing. A kinky one night stand if you like."

She did rather like, but..."You said, you played differently from Mark?"

"Yes. I like pretend games. We'll both dress up. I've got your costume ready up stairs. Finish your tea and then I want you to go up, shower and dress in what I've laid out. "

Annie nodded and wrapped her hands round her mug. This *was* going to be different. "Okay if I ask what the costume is?"

"Of course, we're not playing yet. We'll do a master and troublesome maidservant routine." His eyes twinkled. "I rather think you're going to give me no end of trouble."

'"And you'll enjoy every bit of it!"

"So will you." He was right about that! "Anything special you want?"

He wasn't talking about a chocolate biccy with her tea. She took a drink, it was still too hot but she needed to gather her thoughts. She'd finally become used to talking to Mark, but Tom... Oh, hell! Why hesitate? Tom Baldwin knew things about her, her own mother would never guess at! "I like feeling utterly helpless."

"I'll make sure of it."

She swallowed again, mostly air this time. "What do you want?" she asked–when she finally got her throat wet enough to speak.

"You know what turns me up to full power? Having you beg. Beg me not to beat you, even though we both know I will. Beg me to fuck you."

"Okay!" And Tom wondered if he could turn her on! He didn't need to worry! She was turned on, up, and, almost over.

"Smashing. We'll start when you finish your tea."

She was tempted to chug-a-lug it down in one swallow.

Chapter Four

Tea finished, Tom took her upstairs, stripped her naked, and left her, saying he had to get ready and would meet her in the kitchen. Alone, Annie looked around. The decorators had been busy in his guest quarters. She could happily spend a week in the bathroom, complete with sauna, tiled walls and floor, and a sunken whirlpool. Pity all she had to do was shower. But she did her best with the scented shower foam and shampoo, drying off with thick towels from the heated rail and perching on a satin-covered buttonback chair as she dried her hair with the hair dryer waiting on the marble counter top. She'd have lingered, but wanted to try on the costume she glimpsed as Tom led her through the bedroom.

The costume was simple: a loose shift, a drawstring blouse with puff sleeves and a full skirt with attached petticoats and white starched apron. No underwear–hardly a surprise. The costume went on easily enough. Annie took a few minutes deciding whether or not to wear the blouse off her shoulders, but decided not. If Tom wanted her showing her cleavage, he could demand it. She gave her hair a last ruffle to stop it drying flat, and wondered why she bothered. By the time they finished it would be slick with sweat.

Time to be a troublesome maid.

She almost gaped when she saw Tom.

He must have raided a studio wardrobe department for his get up: tight knee breeches tucked into shiny back boots, a snowy white shirt with full sleeves and a gathered neck tie, and a frock coat in a glorious velvet the color of rich claret. Tom definitely had to go into period drama when his series stopped. She looked him over from dark brown hair to shiny black boots and smiled–or did until she noticed the black, leather-covered riding crop in his hand.

"At last, Annie! And well may you stop smiling. I demand an explanation!"

What was she supposed to do now? "Tom, I…"

"Is that how you address your employer?"

Yes, of course. Troublesome maidservant. She lowered her eyes. "I'm sorry, Sir."

"Sorry is not good enough, Annie. I've spoken to you before about your carelessness. Kindly explain this!" He slapped the end of the crop on table beside the tea tray, sending the cups rattling.

Annie jumped at the noise. The tray was full of fine, bone china cups, one missing a handle, another in several pieces, and a saucer broken in two. So, this was it. Careless housemaid breaks the best china and…a wild thrill ran straight to her cunt as she thought of the crop in Tom's hand. "I'm sorry, Sir, really I am! I didn't mean to, Sir! " She even managed a little whine as she tailed off.

"That, Annie, is what you told me last time! Remember my warning?" Getting into the spirit of the scene, Annie bit her lip and hung her head. "Another instance of ham handedness, and you'd be dismissed," Annie looked up. His brows creased over a pair of hard eyes. "Without a character reference." That threat would have meant unemployment and the prospect of life on the streets. Enough to put dread in any servant's heart. "Please, Sir! My blind mother depends on my salary!"

"She can go to the workhouse, Annie."

They were crossing time periods a bit, but what the heck? "I'll do anything, Sir! Anything! Please don't turn me out." She managed a little sob. It was only half-put on. Tom picked up the crop and gently tapped it against the palm of his hand. Wasn't this what she wanted? But the crop had a nasty-looking leather loop at the end. It would not feel anything like her soft suede whip. Or would it?

"Anything?" Tom raised a carefully plucked eyebrow. "Offenses such as yours require earnest penitence."

Heaven help some poor housemaid in this position for real! Tom was leering like a villainous employer right out of Victorian erotica. "I'm very penitent, Sir. Really I am!" To add weight to her act, Annie dropped to her knees and bowed her head. It felt so god-awful wonderful, she shivered with anticipation. Shiny black boots shifted slightly in her line of vision. Tom's hand rested on the crown of her head and a great yearning for whatever awaited rushed over her like a warm tide.

"I'll accept your penitence, Annie. You've been a good, obedient and loyal maid, but you must change your careless habits. This time I will merely deduct the cost of the china from your wages."

'Thank you Sir." Was that it! No. The crop tapped her shoulder. There was more--much more she hoped.

"You must willingly accept your chastisement without complaint. Do you understand?"

"Yes, Sir. I will." Her mouth went dry. He meant she was not to cry out. She could be silent--if he didn't hit too hard. This was play, wasn't it?

"Very well, Annie. But first, you must demonstrate your true penitence."

"Sir?"

"Before I mete out the whipping you so rightly deserve, you will suck my cock."

Annie nodded, and smiled down at the toes of Tom's polished boots. That would be no hardship. "Yes, Sir!"

Tom's legs were lean and long in his more usual tropical wool or twill. Heck, they looked sexy in blue jeans, and marvelous in shorts. But there was something about tan knee breeches that took her breath away. They literally molded his thighs, and clung to every curve--including the growing bulge in this groin. "I'm waiting, Annie," he said in a tone that brooked no delay.

Annie moved to oblige.

A zip would have been handy, but no, his darn costume was historically accurate. She fumbled with tiny concealed buttons and tapes before getting her hands on his cock. It was warm in her fingers, and already hard. It took an effort not to smile, but Tom was watching her every move. If she had been truly in danger of ejection onto the streets without a reference, she'd be anxious, and terrified her efforts wouldn't please. Fine, Annie the housemaid would do her darndest.

She took a deep breath, opened her mouth and swallowed him.

His thighs trembled under her hands

There was no way she could smile now. She was filled. Her mouth stretched by Tom's magnificent cock. She had to concentrate on her breathing and fight gagging, but in a few seconds, while Tom stayed accommodatingly still, she relaxed her throat to his size. Pulling back just a little, Annie swirled her tongue around the tender, smooth skin covering the head of his cock. She hesitated over the tiny opening and tasted the sweetness of his pre-come.

Her knees wobbled as the desire bursting deep in her cunt took over her mind. This felt so right! Tom's hands enclosed her head. His touch wasn't Mark's. But it was enough to remind her that she was Tom's servant, his bottom, and soon she'd be feeling his harsh touch on her body. That thought sent her cunt creaming. She was so needy it was pathetic–and wonderful. A week of only phone sex left her yearning for a master's touch, and maidservant Annie longed to do Tom's bidding.

She fluttered her tongue around the ridge just below the head of his cock, flicking back and forth over the knot of skin that met the rim on the underside. Tom's grip on her hair tightened. Annie the maidservant would have long hair, to be pulled and twisted for this purpose. Life as a real servant held no appeal, but penitent Annie the housemaid aka Annie Cavendish, whimpered with pleasure.

"Quiet!" Tom ordered, but eased his hand away. "Save your energies for pleasing me, not moaning. "

That upped her need several notches, but perfected her concentration. Breathing steadily she pursed her lips and sucked him in to the hilt. Holding her mouth steady a few seconds, she dragged her lips along the length of Tom's cock until they brushed the raised flesh below his cock head. She eased her lips into a tight circle and rocked her mouth back and forth over his warm ridge. As she sucked his cock back into her mouth, he let out a long, slow moan, and holding her head firmly in both hands, pulled away.

"Enough," he said, stepping back. His beautiful cock was rampant, pink with arousal, moist with her saliva, and right at eye level. It was impossible not to stare.

"Look at me," he ordered.

Annie looked up to Tom's flushed face. His eyes had lost some of their harshness, and his breathing was as fast as hers, but calmed as she watched him reach for the crop lying beside the broken crockery.

His breathing might have slowed. Hers sped up as he ran the leather loop around the neckline of her blouse. "Annie, I do believe you showed appropriate penitence. Are you prepared to receive your well-merited chastisement?" Her reply seemed lodged in her impossibly dry throat. "Are you, Annie?" he repeated.

If possible, her cunt flowed faster at his question. Every trace of moisture in her body seemed pooled between her legs. Her clit throbbed and a sweet ache gnawed between her thighs. She wanted this, she needed it, and she so dreaded it. Tom's face resumed its irate master look. "I am waiting for your consent to beat you, Annie!"

Mark had never spoken so bluntly, but her tongue had never glued itself into paralysis before. Unable to speak, she nodded.

"I wish to hear it from your lovely, fuckable lips, Annie. Are you ready?" The storybook apparition in red velvet waited.

"Yes, Sir," she managed through stiff lips. "I'm ready." Her entire body shuddered, from relief at getting the words out, or fear of what followed, she'd never know nor care.

Tom's hand on her arm, pulled her to her feet. "First you wash all the cups and saucers," he said. "When they are dry and put in order, then you present yourself to me."

Without another word, he strode out, breeches still hanging open, cock stiff and ready, and his frock coat swirling as he turned away.

Chapter Five

Washing up! She was ready to scream with frustration! Tom knew exactly how to tease a submissive. This was going to be wonderful agony. But judging by the sight of his ramrod-stiff cock as he walked past, it wasn't going to easy for him either.

But she was the one stuck with the dishes.

Talk about getting into the spirit of the play! Darn him! A wide tape sealing the dishwasher made it clear, it was hands in the suds to wash up. Tom had been busy while she showered. He'd also covered up the hot tap. Housemaid Annie was back in boil water for washing days. She filled the kettle, concluding she was lucky to have the gas stove within bounds and she wasn't expected to go outside to a pump.

Waiting for the darn kettle to boil, Annie piled the cups--broken pieces and all--into the sink, and stole the chance to sit down. Might as well snatch a moment while she could. It would be rigorous play in a very short while.

This watched pot boiled at amazing speed. Washing, rinsing, and drying four cups and saucers plus broken pieces wasn't exactly time-consuming or onerous. Her arousal had cooled, just a tad, but her anxiety meter had risen several notches, and Tom was waiting. She could leave now, just tell him goodbye, change back into street clothes, and call Mark to pick her up. It would be so easy--and utterly impossible. She was alive with expectations. Whatever Tom was about to deal out, she desired. Every nerve quivered with anticipation and dread. No way would she miss this for the world.

She wiped her hands, smoothed her apron, and walked into the sitting room. "I'm ready, Sir," she announced.

"Are you?" He was sitting in one of the wing chairs, one leg over the arm of the chair while he so carelessly flicked the end of the crop against his boot. Would the narrow leather make a similar sound on her skin? She forced her gaze from the swinging crop to Tom. He looked like the villain in a novel. He'd tossed the velvet coat over the back of the sofa, the ends of his cravat hung loose, and he'd unbuttoned the neck of the shirt and rolled up his sleeves, as if for action. Action on her hide!

To add to the scene, she bit her lip, and managed a penitent sob. "The washing up's all done, Sir."

"Did you break any more china?"

Was she meant to? "Oh! No! Sir! I was as careful as can be."

"Lucky for your bottom, isn't it? I won't have to add any extra. Maybe you've learned your lesson at last." He shook his head. "I just can't have carelessness, it just won't do at all. Now..." He paused as if waiting, and Annie remembered his parting command.

"How should I present myself, Sir?"

"On your knees!" As she hit the carpet, he went on, "and I'm disappointed I had to wait. You should have been down on the floor the minute you entered the room."

She would have if his appearance, like a profligate-about-to-be-reformed-hero in a novel, hadn't distracted her. "I apologize, Sir." Utterly! With the leather loop swinging in and out of her line of vision.

"I believe you, Annie." Tom went on, "and since you sucked my cock with such devotion, I will be generous. I'll warm your bottom up by spanking before I lay on you properly."

Her stomach sunk towards her ready cunt. Mark always claimed a warm-up spanking made the flogger or crop easier to bear. Annie had never been convinced, but now was not the time to debate that point.

"You want to safeword out, Annie?"

It took a second to grasp what he'd asked. "No!" she almost shouted. "Oh! No!"

Tom was smirking now. "I thought not, but just to be sure, what is your safe word?"

"Annette Sophia Cavendish."

"Good!" Tom stood up. "Let's get started." The tops of his boots and his twill-encased thighs filled her entire line of vision. He'd refastened his breeches, but the bulge in his groin proved he was ready and willing. "Bend over the back of the sofa."

She needed his help to stand. Her legs wobbled and her blood pressure thrummed in her ears. She wanted this so much. She feared what he was about to do. Tom had a strong right arm. She remembered how he wielded the belt before. The front door was just yards away. The phone was closer. If she called Mark…

Annie walked across to the sofa, knelt on the chintz cushions and arranged herself over the back.

"No, Annie. Facing the other way. Walk to the back of the sofa and bend over forwards."

She should have asked for clarification. Seven nervous steps had her around the sofa and facing Tom. She looked up at his eyes, brimming with the same anticipation that rippled in her cunt, and remembered, he wanted her to beg.

"Oh, Sir," she began, adding a little sob. "I'm scared, Sir! Please Sir, don't hurt me!"

He raised one eyebrow and looked. In silence.

Annie bit her lip.

Tom tapped the crop against his boot and waited.

"Sir?" she began again, a nervous coil forming in her stomach. He'd asked her to beg, hadn't he?

"Annie, I will count to three. If by then you are not bent over and ready for punishment, I will go up stairs and fetch my cane!" She believed him. "One!

Two!" She tipped herself over to grasp the sofa pillows as he said, "Three!"

The side of her face rubbed against Tom's discarded velvet jacket. As she inhaled the combined scents of Eau Sauvage and Tom, his hands cupped her buttocks through her skirt and petticoats. He squeezed. Annie felt every fingertip through the layers of cloth. She swallowed hard and took a deep breath. It was beginning.

But not immediately.

For several long seconds, Tom contented himself with kneading and squeezing until every centimeter of her bottom felt embossed with Tom's fingerprints. He'd still not touched her skin.

A surprised whimper escaped her lips as the side of his hand swept up the crease of her arse. "Silence, Annie!" Tom snapped. "I'll gag you if you can't control your noise."

Annie bit her lip. She bet Tom knew exactly how much she hated the gag. Trust Mark to share every little snippet. She sighed from deep in her diaphragm, and hoped to hell that didn't count as noise.

Tom stepped away. She felt the loss of his touch as certainly as she'd responded to his fondling. "Don't move, Annie. Whatever you do!" She was grasping the front edge of the sofa with her fingertips.

"Here, look after this for me." He dropped the crop onto the cushion, so it lay alongside her forearm. A swift adjustment, and the loop end was pushed under her hand. "And this!" He shoved the handle of her suede whip into her other hand. So much for planning on using it on him! It was going to grace her hide! Perhaps. Which would he use? Both? The hard, black length of leather, or the soft stingy tresses of purple suede? Didn't leather hurt more than suede? Didn't it depend on how hard he hit? No point in crossing that bridge yet. She'd find out soon enough.

It might not be that soon. The carved clock over the mantelpiece clicked away the minutes, and Tom didn't return. She was tempted to straighten up and ease her back and the tension in her thighs, but he'd told her to wait, and wait she would...but how much longer?

All night if he chose.

Remembering Mark's instructions on relaxing, Annie closed her eyes and breathed slowly and deeply. If it worked with bondage, it would surely work bent double over a sofa back that became less comfortable with every passing minute. She let her shoulders and arms go heavy, relaxed her knees as best she could, and let her mind float free. She succeeded so well, she was halfway to dozing when Tom thumped her bottom. It wasn't hard, nowhere near what she expected, but brought her out of her reverie with a yelp.

"Tut, tut," Tom said, the chuckle only too apparent in his voice. "Noisy little housemaid, aren't you, Annie?" His hand smoothed her arse, almost as if he were stroking her. "You'll have to do better if you wish to remain in my employ!"

He grabbed her by the waist with both hands and shifted her forward. She managed to contain her cry–-but only just. Talk about awkward! She was bent at the hips, not her waist, the edge of the back pressing the crease of the thighs and her face and chest flattened against the sofa. She was now clutching for the carpet, not the cushions, and her toes were barely touching the floor. The end of the crop pressed one breast through her thin blouse and the tresses of the pussy whip tickled her arm. Talk about awkward, uncomfortable and exposed! Her arse was poised, bent, and taut. Her thigh muscles stretched as she fought to keep her toes on the floor. With one movement, Tom had her skirt and petticoats over her head, blocking out light and muffling sound.

Tom's breeches brushed her bare legs, as his hands ran up her inner thighs and pulled them apart. He was standing between her legs and lifting them. Her feet were off the floor, the inside of her knees rubbing his waist. She'd been uncomfortable and helpless earlier. Now she was as completely at his mercy as if she'd been tied up or cuffed to the furniture.

He stepped closer, spreading her wider. She was secure. No chance of falling. No chance of going anywhere. Between her chest on the seat of the sofa and her legs tensed against Tom's side, she was more or less comfortable, and exposed utterly.

"Ready Annie?" Tom asked. As he spoke, the first slap landed. Even with her ears covered, the smack resounded against her arse. The echo seemed to hang in the quiet room. "Remember, not a sound until I give you permission." Down came his hand again.

He wasn't hitting hard. It was nowhere near as severe as her first spanking from Mark, but it was thorough. Slowly but surely, Tom covered every inch of her naked arse and thighs. The sting faded to a tingle, but built up layer on layer until her skin burned, and her cunt throbbed with need.

"Love the way you color up," Tom said, not even pausing in his spanks. "Quite the most delicious shade, almost like a Maiden's Blush rose." He chuckled–obviously at his own wit–as a harder slap on her tender right cheek elicited a little gasp. "No," he murmured, "more like Tivoli, if you ask me." She wasn't asking him. She was trying to contain her moans. "Know about roses do you, Annie?" Not much and cared less. How much longer? She'd twice now bitten her lip keeping quiet. He might not hit hard, but Tom was thorough. He gave her four more slaps. "That should be enough for now."

She was not about to argue. The dull throb and sting radiated from her burning bottom. Seemed every nerve ending tingled. Her clit throbbed to the point of hurt. She needed release. As Tom lowered her legs, she rubbed herself against the back of the sofa to ease the ache in her clit.

"No, indeed!" The hard slap made her yelp. "Dirty little girl! Rubbing yourself against the furniture! That's not how you behave! I've a good mind to throw you out the door this instant!"

"No, Sir! Please! Don't. I'll be good. I promise! " she called though her layers of petticoats. She was Annie the maid, terrified of her future.

Another slap on the second cheek she was almost ready for, but her aching need brought tears to her eyes. "Behave yourself! Or I'll strap you in a chastity belt and never give you release!"

Would he? She didn't doubt it for one minute. She tried to ignore the incessant throbbing in her clit. She whimpered as he reached between her legs and pushed fingers into her cunt. How many? Aroused as she was, he could have his fist up there and she'd be happy. But just as her cunt muscles clenched with satisfaction against his fingers, he withdrew. "Wait, Annie," he said, "your time to come will come!"

Very funny!

Tom thought so. He chuckled. He wouldn't chuckle like that when Claudine laid into him next time--but that was in the future. Right now it was her body on the receiving end. Her nipples were hard and hurting from being squashed against the cushions. Her cunt ran with arousal, and her clit hurt almost as much as her arse...and that was just a warm up. She shivered.

"Going to break any more crockery?" Tom asked, his hand resting on her arse, as if enjoying the heat.

"'Oh no, Sir. Never."

"I'm delighted to know my correction is yielding results. Let's get it over with then. Nothing like laying it on when the flesh is warm. We don't want you cooling off, do we?" She couldn't see any problem with that but... " Want to have my crop or your flogger?"

He was asking? "Whatever pleases you, Sir."

"No, Annie. You must choose. I insist. "

Wonderful! The familiar flogger or the unknown crop? Decisions! Decisions! Clenching clammy palms tight, Annie whispered. "The flogger, please, Sir."

His hand caressed her left butt cheek. "You want the flogger, not the crop?"

"Yes, Sir!"

Softly he stroked down her thigh to the back of her knee. "I'll beat you, you do understand, don't you? This is punishment."

"Yes, Sir, I understand."

"Why am I punishing you, Annie?"

"Because I was careless, Sir, and broke your pretty china."

"Yes, and now you will receive your just desserts!" He gave a little slap. It made more nose than hurt, but sent her heart racing. "Very well, at your request, my dear, the flogger it is." He stroked her other, still warm cheek. "But first!" He grabbed her by her shoulders and yanked her to her feet. "I want you naked!" He spun her to face him and ripped open her blouse before she had time to process his words.

She gasped as the thin muslin gave way, exposing her breasts. She looked up into Tom's face. His eyes glimmered with a deep fire, but his face was set and stern. At her cry he creased his brows until a furrow appeared between his eyes. "Not resisting are you, Annie? This is my right as your indulgent employer!" His hand squeezed her left breast. There was no gentleness in his touch. He pinched and pressed until she bit her lip. He squeezed her nipple. Life as a servant had to have been the pits!

"Sir! You're hurting me!"

"I haven't even started!"

Rape had never been one of her fantasies, but feeling Tom's breath on her face, and his fingers on her breasts, a hideous excitement roiled deep inside. It was play, it was terrifying, and she wanted to be dragged along with his imagination.

"Please, don't hurt me, Sir. No!" She tried to pull away, but his body pinned her against the sofa.

He gave a laugh, worthy of the worst villain in melodrama, and tipped her backwards on the sofa. She struggled to get up, as he pressed her legs apart with his knee, but she was half upside down, with her head on the seat cushions. Her movement was hampered by her skirts and his grip on her thighs. She managed to lift her head and shoulders, Tom threw up her skirts, and she found herself struggling with yards of fabric.

"What do we have here?" Another nasty chuckle! "A naked quim! You naughty girl!" His hand cupped her mound. At her cry, the heel of his hand ground into the moist flesh around her clit. "What fun I'll have fucking you, Annie. But first!" He pulled her upright. Her skirts fell back to her calves, but there was no way she could cover her breasts. Not that she wanted to. The thrill of power when Tom ogled them was not to be missed. But now... "I'll fuck you," he promised, "maybe even bugger you, but only after you feel the flogger on your luscious body."

She was creaming now. She wanted this to go on forever. Excitement rose to fever pitch as he pulled the tatters of her blouse off her shoulders, and asked, "Will you resist me, Annie? Should I tie you down?"

Please! She held back. He wanted her begging, not enthusiastic. "Oh, Sir, I'm scared. I can't stay still if you hurt me!" She yearned to fight against his restraints.

He grabbed her wrist and dragged her to the middle of the room. "Better make sure, hadn't I?" Pulling out one of her discarded thigh-highs from his breeches pocket, he yanked her arms behind her and lashed her wrists together. "That should take care of things!" The binding was loose enough to be comfortable, but with arms pinioned behind, her balance was unsteady, and she doubted she could walk without his hand to steady her. "Wait there!" He left her standing while he walked back to the sofa to retrieve her flogger.

And she'd actually planned on using it on him! No, this was far better, she wanted the kiss of the fine suede tresses and the glorious sting on her flesh. Was he going to make her wait?

No!

Grinning, he trailed the soft tails across her bared breasts. She sighed with pleasure, and closed her eyes to concentrate on the sensation of suede dragged across her skin. But eyes closed, her balance went, and she'd have fallen if Tom hadn't grabbed her by the waist and set her upright.

"Tut! Tut! That won't do. Now, how can I make sure you stay still?" He pursed his lips as if concentrating. Where was he going to restrain her? One of the overhead or vertical oak beams perhaps? How? She didn't much care, just as long as he made her helpless. "Hah!" He gave a nasty chuckle. "Perfect." Wrapping his strong hand around her upper arm, Tom propelled her towards a Victorian fainting couch under the window. Leaving her standing, he dragged the couch away from the wall, walked back to her with a self-satisfied smile and yanked down her skirts and petticoats. The elastic waistbands gave easily and she was naked, surrounded by a billowing circle of skirts and petticoats. "Upsadaisy!" he said with a grin as he held her arm to help her step away from the last of her costume, and spun her around and tipped her backwards.

Annie yelped as she landed on the couch, arms pinned fast by her own weight. Before she had a chance to struggle, Tom grabbed an ankle and strapped it to the couch. Definitely planned! She heard the scritch of velcro as he fastened her leg to one side, and moments later fixed the other leg on the opposite side. She was wide open, feet off the floor so she had little chance of righting herself, her own weight holding her arms fast behind her.

Helpless! Her body responded with even more heightened desire. She yearned for the kiss of her flogger, and if he left her tied like this, it was a good, solid fuck that awaited her, not a buggering. "Yes!" he muttered, "Nicely helpless, aren't you. Ready for it, Annie?"

She'd been ready for the last hour! But whispered, "Oh, Sir!" in a little voice, that faded to a sigh as suede tresses kissed between her breasts down to her bare pussy.

He lost the irate employer look and gave her a grin that was pure Tom. "Don't go anywhere while I get ready," he said, and sat down on an upright chair a few feet away, but not before draping the flogger across her belly, so the handle rested between her breasts and the tresses kissed her denuded pussy. With every breath she took the suede thongs shifted and teased her sensitive flesh.

She was tempted to rock her hips, to shift the tresses closer and deeper as well as easing the pressure on her still-tender bottom, but since Tom was watching her intently, even as he yanked off one boot and then the other, she abandoned the idea.

Composing her mind, and calming a little might be a very good idea, but hard to do as Tom removed his breeches right in front of her eyes.

He was beautiful! No wonder she'd gone ape-crazy for him that day in Cornwall. She couldn't help smiling as his erect cock sprang free of his clothing and aimed at her. Soon-she hoped. She was grinning as he tossed his shirt aside and faced her in naked glory.

"Something amuses you?" he asked, reverting to his irate master role.

"No, Sir. I'm just awed by your beauty!"

Obviously not in the script! He stared for a minute, grinned and got right back in role. "I am delighted with your respectful admiration, Annie. Show me your respectful submission. Remember you may not climax, if you reach that point, you know what to say."

She did. "Edge, Sir."

"Good," he said, coming to stand beside her. "Let's see how long you can last." As he grasped the handle of the flogger, his fingertips brushed her breasts. She couldn't hold back the sigh. "Yes," he said. "I'd like to hear you sing." He raised the flogger and swept the tresses across her breasts.

She gasped, again and again, as he worked her body. He wasn't beating. He was punishing her with caresses and teasing. How long could she last? Ages! She wanted this to go on forever. Tom swished the flogger down her belly and gently flicked her pussy, moving lower to tease the inside of her thighs, her knees, her shins, even the soles of her feet before returning to the soft sensitive skin of her inner thighs, but all the while avoiding the damp throbbing skin around her clit.

Chapter Six

Tom was a master of the tease, an expert at arousal. How much longer could she last? Did she want to? As the tresses swished back and forth across her belly and thighs, and her arm muscles fought against her bonds, sensations peaked even higher. Her hips shifted involuntarily. Every nerve ending sprung alive with sensation. Her mind fuzzed-out in a haze of pleasure. She was spiraling into white heat arousal. A stray tail across her pussy sent her mind and body reeling. "Edge!" she cried.

"Annie!" The flogger hit the floor as Tom rested one knee on the reclining couch and bent over her. Warm fingers parted her cunt lips and Tom bent and kissed her clit. She screamed with pleasure as his mouth closed down and his fingers pressed deep inside her. Tom's fingers curled, catching her G spot, and she shot into orbit. Her hips bucked and her head rocked from side to side as Tom's mouth and fingers released a cascade of climaxes, each seeming harder and higher than the last. Annie finally collapsed, soaked in sweat, her hips still rocking as her breasts heaved with labored breathing.

"Dear heaven, Annie!" Tom's voice was close to awed, as he lifted her shoulders. "Hold on love, gotta undo you!"

Her hands were free in seconds. "How," she gasped as she sagged back and he rubbed her wrists, "did you undo it so easily?"

"Told you I was a Boy Scout! Slip knot!" He kissed her left breast. "Satisfactory, Ma'am?"

"Magnificent!" She was smirking and didn't give a hoot. "You are incredible, Tom!"

"Wasn't all me," he shrugged. "I just followed the script.

It wasn't 'just' anything. She'd had the climax of the life, and he…She smiled at his rampant cock. "Isn't it your turn?" Surely they hadn't insisted he not come.

"Yeah!" He grinned. "Just let me untie your legs, and I'll give you a thorough frigging."

"No!" He looked downright disappointed. That wasn't what she intended. "It's okay, Tom. I want you too." And soon. "But leave my legs tied. I like being restrained."

"Anything to oblige!" He stood up, and smiled down at her spread body. "Mmm. Just a tick!" He stepped back to the sofa and grabbed one of the soft pillows and tucked it under her hips. "That makes you nicely available. I'd tie those arms down but I think they've had enough for one session." She wouldn't disagree. Her wrists still smarted. "Tell you what," He gently took a wrist in each hand and raised her arms over her head so they rested against the end of the couch. "pretend they're tied. Don't move them.

"He trailed his hand down her body. "Wanna good fucking, Annie?"

Please! But he wanted begging. "Please, please! Please, Tom, fuck me, I need it so much. I need you. I need your big cock in my cunt. I want a fucking. Please, frig me! Fuck me! Fill me!"

"Since you asked so nicely!" He chuckled, as he knelt between her legs. Holding her hips steady, he pressed his cock against her cunt opening and asked, "Sure you want a fuck, Annie?"

"Yes!" She half-screamed as he thrust deep.

She sighed with slow longing as he slowly withdrew–almost completely–before plunging back deep, pressing hard against her cervix before easing out again. Their previous fuck had been fast and furious. This was slow, sweet, and delicious. Seemed he could continue forever as he slowly but surely brought her back to the edge. As his hot, hard cock pistoned within, she rocked in time with his thrusts, pressing herself forward so the force of his cock stimulated her clit, and she moaned and cried with pleasure. When she thought she could take no more, Tom cried out, "Annie!" And drove in deep. His final thrust ripped her free from her mind, as her body raced in yet another wild climax, and she screamed Mark's name aloud.

Tom reached over and untied her legs as she still lay panting, her heart clenched with shock and horror at what she'd just done.

"Alright, Annie?" Tom asked as he lifted her ankles and placed her legs on the couch before lying down beside her. He was going to be noble and polite about it, and that made her feel worse.

"I'm sorry, Tom."

"Whatever for?"

He obviously hadn't noticed in the throes of his own climax. Or had he? She took a deep breath. "Tom, didn't you notice? I called out the wrong name." What if he hadn't heard? "I'm sorry."

"Oh, Annie!" He gave a little sigh and pulled her close. "Don't worry about it! I heard. So what?"

"A bit tactless isn't it? Calling out the wrong name in the moment of passion!"

"Who says it was the wrong name?" He patted her shoulder and dropped a kiss on her head. "Annie, this is play, not passion, right?" She frowned. Was it? Yes, she supposed so but... "You're Mark's as surely as I belong to Claudine. You and I fancied each other, had the hots for each other, and you chuffed me utterly asking for me as a birthday present, but I had no illusions you loved me, and I hope to heaven you don't think you love me-at least not in that way!"

Some unique post-coital conversation! Annie pondered a few moments and looked sideways at Tom: hair plastered to his head, face still flushed and sweat glistening on his broad shoulders. He was lovely, but he was right, he wasn't Mark. Either this whole thing was totally insane, or the sanest thing in the history of men and women.

She hugged him, "Tom, I do love you, truly, but I'm in love with Mark. Make sense?"

"Yes, love," he replied. "Completely. You were pretty fantastic yourself you know that?" He gave a thoroughly self-satisfied, male smirk. "I think we did damn well together. I might just ask for you for Christmas."

"You think Claudine will agree?"

"She either will, or tell me 'no' and beat the hide off me for impudence. Either way, I win!"

He was right. Everything was right. The world and her life were perfect. She shut her eyes and leaned into his warm body.

"Hey!" Tom pulled away and stood up. "You're ready to pass out on me. Time for bed." And scooped her up in his arms.

Definitely an experience worth having. Annie rested her face against his chest and listened to his heartbeat as he crossed the room and pushed open double doors at the far end.

So this was Tom's bedroom! She looked around as he sat her down on the edge of his bed.

"Like it?" he asked as she stared at the pale gray walls, darker gray bed covers, and the original art on the walls.

"It's so you!" she said, "But not the least what I expected."

He grinned. "What did you expect? Black leather duvet covers? Chains? Or draped velvet on the walls?"

"I don't know what I expected, but this is lovely!"

"Good! Won't give you bad dreams. Look, hop into bed, and I'll get you a snack. You ate almost nothing at dinner, and you burned up a zillion calories tonight."

Tom was consideration itself: giving her a tee-shirt to sleep in and fluffing up pillows behind her back before nipping back to the kitchen and returning with a tray laden with champagne in an ice bucket, caviar, and Melba toast.

"Sure you don't have a treasure of a servant lurking in a pantry somewhere waiting to put this together?" Annie asked.

"No such luck! I bought the caviar and toast in Selfridges and the champagne from a place in Curzon Street. Let's see what you think of it." He eased out the cork and poured two glasses, handing her one. "Happy Birthday, Annie."

Annie sipped, feeling the bubbles burst against her face as she tilted the flute and drank. "Wonderful!"

"Now let's tuck into the caviar." Tom heaped a square of toast with caviar and little mounds of chopped egg and onion, and handed it to her. She bit down savoring the inspired combination of salty caviar, sharp onion, and the smooth texture of finely chopped egg.

Champagne and caviar was not her usual bedtime snack, but nothing could have tasted better. She reached for a second piece of toast. And a third.

"You've gone very quiet, " Tom said, heaping a little mound of egg yolk onto his caviar.

"I was just wondering," she grinned at him over the edge of her champagne flute. "if I tell them at school, I spent my birthday eating caviar in bed with Tom Baldwin! Will they believe me?"

"Would you want them to?"

Annie shook her head. "No, what's between us isn't for public consumption."

"Right," Tom replied. "Just between us and our dominants."

"Yea!"

"You're missing Mark?"

She was. Another man would be offended at the knowledge, but… "I'll be glad to see him."

"They'll both be here in the morning. Coming for brunch they said. Here, you finish this." He drained the last of the champagne into her glass. "Here's to a lifetime of happy birthdays."

They scraped the caviar bowl clean and brushed up the stray crumbs of toast from the sheets, before snuggling down to sleep, spooned together like old lovers, or close friends.

"Sleep well," Tom whispered in her ear. "I've got a surprise for you in the morning."

Even that wasn't enough to keep her awake. Between exhaustion, satiation and champagne, she was asleep in minutes.

Tom lay awake listening to her breath. He hoped to hell Mark realized what a gem he had. Annie was fantastic, responsive and smashing. And he had her for a few more hours yet. He'd make the most of it.

Chapter Seven

Annie drifted between sleeping and waking, remembering last night, and looking forward to Mark's arrival. She ought to get up, or at least open her eyes and check the time, but Tom's bed was so comfortable and she wasn't one hundred percent certain how to look him in the eye this morning. Last night had been wild, fun and most definitely all-around satisfying but what now? She wasn't too sure about facing Tom over cornflakes.

"Annie?" The mattress sagged. Tom kissed her softly on the cheek.

"Mmm?" She rolled onto her back and opened her eyes. With the morning sun casting lights in his hair, Tom was a sight to wake up to. "Hello."

"I brought you a cup of tea."

It was an act of such ordinary kindness she couldn't help smiling. Last night had been kink and caviar, not Darjeeling and a couple of Lincoln Creams. "Thanks, Tom!"

"Slept well?"

"Marvelously! Must have been tired out or something."

"Mark told me to use you well."

The smirk was totally intentional. "I think you did."

"I'm not finished yet."

She almost slopped tea on his linen sheets. "I see." Downright lie--she didn't. What now?

Tom leaned back against the foot of the bed, legs stretched out, and grinned. "They're not due for another two hours, and I've yet to give you my birthday present."

"What was last night?"

"That was Mark and Claudine's effort. This morning is mine."

"I gather a cup of tea isn't it?"

"No way, Sweetheart. I have something unforgettable for you, my love. Drink up!" As if she wanted to now! On the other hand she was thirsty as dry sand after all her sweating last night. She took another sip and eyed Tom over the rim of the cup. He looked as beautiful tousled in the morning as he did groomed and polished. A little less threatening than in his frock coat and breeches, but every bit as exciting. He'd pulled on a light silk dressing gown that hid absolutely nothing. He was hard, ready, and bursting for it, and she'd be a fool to turn down his offer. "Don't take too long," he said, his hand smoothing up and down her leg, "I don't want to have to hurry."

Neither did she. If he was offering her good morning sex, she wanted a slow sunrise not a quickie. Annie drank the tea in a couple of swallows and left the biscuits for later. Much later. She put the cup down, thinking she'd never look at a bone china cup and saucer quite the same again. "I'm ready Big Tom. What's it to be?"

He yanked down the bedclothes, pulled off her tee-shirt, and surveyed her nakedness with definite appreciation. His hands eased over her breasts and down her belly until his fingers smoothed her pussy. He opened her and slid a finger in deep. "Luscious and ready. All set, I think!"

For what? He stood up, took her hand, and pulled to her feet. "Come on, Annie." He led her across the deep pile carpet and pulled back floor-length curtains she'd thought covered French windows.

They didn't. Behind them was a double door, with a touch pad operated lock. "To keep the charlady out, " Tom said.

When he pushed the door open, she knew why. This was enough to give your average cleaning woman heart palpitations. Here, in Tom's playroom, was everything she'd expected to see last night–only much, much more. It was far bigger than his ample sitting room. Whips, chains, straps and manacles ornamented the walls. Around the room was the most complete collection of whipping horses, benches, stocks, pillories and crosses she'd ever seen. There was even a cage in one corner, and what looked like a rack at the far end.

But what caught her eye and held her complete attention hung in the middle of the room.

"Like it?" Tom asked.

"Is it what I think it is?"

"That depends, but probably."

"A sex swing?" She'd seen pictures in kinky catalogs and a couple of videos in Mark's collection, but that wasn't the same as standing within touching distance, smelling the leather straps and seeing the shiny, new metal holding it together. She had a hard time taking her eyes off it, as it hung from the ceiling and swung gently as Tom tapped it. "Does it really work?"

"Let's find out," he suggested, his voice bursting with excitement.

She couldn't help smiling, "You don't know? You haven't used it?"

"Not so far. Always fancied having one, and decided to splurge since you were coming. Thought you'd like it."

She most likely would but... "Is this part of the script?"

"Not in the least! This morning is for us. My birthday present if you like. To be honest, I've always wanted to have a go on one of these but I just can't see Claudine fooling around on it, and it doesn't work alone.

It obviously wouldn't. "I used to love swinging when I was little. My grandfather even made one to hang in the garage so I could swing on rainy days."

"We don't have to wait for a rainy day."

They didn't. "Want to swing?"

He pulled her close, pressing her against his erection. "What do you think, Annie?"

"That you're hot, hard and handy!" Just to make sure she closed her hand around his cock. Yes! She'd been right on all three.

"Naughty girl! What if I tell Mark you were forward and provocative?"

"He'll probably believe you!" Hand still on Tom's cock she pulled him closer. "Are we standing here all morning, or are we going swinging?"

"I can't do much but stand here while you've got my vital part in a pincer grip!"

Slowly she released her hold. "That better?" He grinned and shook himself. Yes, he was impressive!

"Let's get into this contraption and I'll show you better and best."

Who in their right mind would refuse that invitation? Annie reached for the wide leather strap suspended from the ceiling and tried to work out exactly where her legs and arms went, and exactly how one got into the apparatus without breaking something. Sprains and fractures would rather spoil the moment.

"Here!" Tom held the swing steady and showed her how to put one leg, then the other into her side of the sling. "Keep it still while I hop in."

Easier said than done. This explained why in videos they were always shown swinging, not clambering in. Tom managed after a couple of tries. As he settled into his side of the leather sling, he pressed close and sank deep into her ready cunt.

Her gasp came from deep in her gut. Suspended, as if they were floating in air, he came in deeper and felt harder than ever before.

"Hold tight," he said as he grasped the leather uprights. "Let's swing."

This was not like the playground swings of their childhood! As Tom leaned back to start the swing going, he slipped half out but she leaned forward and took him back in. As she swung, she set the same in and out into motion. Back and forth they went, slowly and gently at first. Tom's eyes went wide. "This is better than I ever imagined. Fantastic!"

Annie was not about to disagree. Wild sensations rushed her mind. Grinning, she swung faster, shifting her hips and shoulders, and watching Tom's face for his reaction. It was all she could have hoped for.

"Hell! Annie! This is some ride!" He laughed, and as the swing slowed sent it going faster.

How long could they keep this up? Ages she hoped! "If this were out of doors we'd feel the wind in our hair." She'd loved that as a child.

"If this were out of doors, we'd get arrested!"

She threw back her head and laughed. "True! I'll just have to do without the wind in my hair."

"I'd think my cock in your cunt is a fair substitute!"

"More than fair! Magnificent!" No lie. As they rocked back and forth, he rubbed against her still-tender clit. She was no doubt smirking like a fool, but didn't give a hoot. If only this could last all morning.

The first soft climax came moments later. "Tom!" she gasped. "That was...incredible!" As she spoke, another small climax fluttered deep in her cunt. "Tom!"

He grinned as if utterly pleased with himself. "Having fun, dear?"

"I'm having orgasms!"

"Aren't they fun?"

The understatement of the new millennium! But she didn't have breath or energy to agree. Another climax came, and another. They were soft and gentle, nowhere like the wild whirlpools of sensation last night, but so sweet and wonderful she wanted to hang here and swing forever.

She worked harder, the swing moved with her, making wider arcs that seemed to pull out the ripples of pleasure that built on each other until they echoed though her body. She felt Tom tense, deep inside her. Every muscle he moved, she responded to. Watching his face, she knew he was coming. She clenched his cock tight with her cunt, and pushed the swing in his direction, they swung back, and as the swing returned her way, he spasmed deep inside her and gasped, "Annie! Ohmigod! Annie!" and came.

Annie pressed down, summoning all her mind and every nerve ending to absorb the sensations. She climaxed. Not a mind-blowing shattering but a sweet wildness rippling through every muscle, nerve and sinew, that even warmed her bones.

They let the swing slow by itself. Tom slumped towards her, sated from his climax. She rested her head against his warm and sweaty chest. Annie kissed him and tasted the saltiness of his sweat on his skin. An overwhelming tenderness and fondness warmed her deep in her heart. Life was wonderful. Tom was good man, a friend, and he was her birthday present. And the lover of her dreams was on his way to take her home. What more could any woman want? She just hoped she never had to explain things to her mother.

"What's so funny?" Tom asked. She shared her last thought. "Don't ever try," he advised. "No one outside ever understands. That's why we stay together. Just our circle. We understand."

True. She leaned up and kissed him. "Thanks Tom. I won't forget this birthday in a hurry."

"You're welcome, Sweetheart. Now talking of hurry, I promised Claudine Eggs Benedict and I'd better have everything ready by the time they get here, or she'll make scrambled eggs on my bottom!"

"Which you'd thoroughly enjoy!" Annie kissed him again. "Let me get a quick shower." The chance to luxuriate in that sybaritic bathroom was not to be missed. "And I'll help."

Chapter Eight

By the time Mark and Claudine pulled up in front of the cottage, Tom and Annie had finished the first pot of coffee. Annie suspected Tom was as unsettled as she felt, but hid it under his relaxed veneer. Annie put the kettle back on to boil, rinsed the press pot and measured out fresh coffee. At the sound of the car on the gravel drive, her hand froze. Slowly, she put down the press pot and took a couple of hesitant steps towards the door. Tom was way faster. He had it open long before Annie reached the middle of the sitting room. But when Mark stepped over the threshold, she ran forward engulfing him in a hug tight enough stun a bear, or leave a boa constrictor breathless.

Her entire being clung to Mark. She needed to feel his arms around her, inhale the scent of his skin, and rest her face against the strong wall of his chest.

His arms enfolded her. His presence relaxed and reassured. "Annie, love," he whispered.

She shut her eyes and let his words and his power wash over her.

"I love you, Mark!"

"I know Annie. The feeling's mutual. " He tilted her face up so their eyes met. "How was the birthday present?"

She blushed so hard her face burned. "Lovely," she replied, "but I'm so happy you're here."

"Hell, Mark, she's lovely when she blushes like that. Don't ever let her grow out of it," Claudine said, and to Annie's utter astonishment, Mark released his hold and Claudine hugged her. "Did my boy give satisfaction?" she asked.

"Several times over!" Annie couldn't hold back the smirk. "No complaints at all!"

"Good thing too!" Claudine looked at Tom, waiting almost nervously. "Behave yourself, did you?"

"Yes, Boss. Followed the script as you wrote it."

Claudine nodded, raising an eyebrow. "And after?"

Tom gave a little bow. "I endeavored to give satisfaction!"

"I bet you did!" She looked from Tom to Annie and back. "Alright you two. We've had an early drive from London. Where's breakfast?"

Between them, Tom and Annie got it on the table in record time. The eggs were perfect, the English muffins--genuine American ones imported and sent down from Harrods--toasted just exactly right, and the ham--from a nearby farm, tastier than anything Annie had ever eaten. Or perhaps it was the company, and the mood, and her very stimulated appetite. She'd seldom ever felt happier. But her contentment boosted up several notches when Mark put down his coffee mug and said, "Annie, let's leave Tom to do the washing up. I want to take you home. I need you naked under me."

She threw Tom an apologetic glance but he just grinned. "Better go Annie. That sounds more like a command than an invitation."

She hoped so, but didn't care which it was. It came from Mark, her lover and the man who knew and understood her utterly.

She stood up. "I'm ready, Mark." For whatever he had waiting.

About the authors:

Dominique Adair, Jennifer Dunne, and Madeleine Oh welcome mail from readers. You can write to them c/o Ellora's Cave Publishing at P.O. Box 787, Hudson, Ohio 44236-0787.

Also by DOMINIQUE ADAIR:

Last Kiss

Also by JENNIFER DUNNE:

Sex Magic
Luck of the Irish anthology with Kate Douglas & Chris Tanglen

Also by MADELEINE OH:

Power Exchange

Why an electronic book?

We live in the Information Age—an exciting time in the history of human civilization in which technology rules supreme and continues to progress in leaps and bounds every minute of every hour of every day. For a multitude of reasons, more and more avid literary fans are opting to purchase e-books instead of paperbacks. The question to those not yet initiated to the world of electronic reading is simply: *why?*

1. *Price.* An electronic title at Ellora's Cave Publishing runs anywhere from 40-75% less than the cover price of the <u>exact same title</u> in paperback format. Why? Cold mathematics. It is less expensive to publish an e-book than it is to publish a paperback, so the savings are passed along to the consumer.

2. *Space.* Running out of room to house your paperback books? That is one worry you will never have with electronic novels. For a low one-time cost, you can purchase a handheld computer designed specifically for e-reading purposes. Many e-readers are larger than the average handheld, giving you plenty of screen room. Better yet, hundreds of titles can be stored within your

new library—a single microchip. (Please note that Ellora's Cave does not endorse any specific brands. You can check our website at www.ellorascave.com for customer recommendations we make available to new consumers.)

3. *Mobility*. Because your new library now consists of only a microchip, your entire cache of books can be taken with you wherever you go.

4. *Personal preferences are accounted for*. Are the words you are currently reading too small? Too large? Too...ANNOYING? Paperback books cannot be modified according to personal preferences, but e-books can.

5. *Innovation*. The way you read a book is not the only advancement the Information Age has gifted the literary community with. There is also the factor of what you can read. Ellora's Cave Publishing will be introducing a new line of interactive titles that are available in e-book format only.

6. *Instant gratification*. Is it the middle of the night and all the bookstores are closed? Are you tired of waiting days—sometimes weeks—for online and offline bookstores to ship the novels you bought? Ellora's Cave Publishing sells instantaneous downloads 24 hours a day, 7 days a week, 365 days a

year. Our e-book delivery system is 100% automated, meaning your order is filled as soon as you pay for it.

Those are a few of the top reasons why electronic novels are displacing paperbacks for many an avid reader. As always, Ellora's Cave Publishing welcomes your questions and comments. We invite you to email us at service@ellorascave.com or write to us directly at: P.O. Box 787, Hudson, Ohio 44236-0787.